ABIGAIL AND MOIRA . . .
A TASTE OF SUGAR,
A BITE OF SPICE!

The van Pelt twins wing it to London, where they get —and give—the royal treatment.

LORD JAMES BARRINGTON thrills Abigail with his magic touch in the august chambers of the House of Lords.

CLARRISA wrestles Moira down to the last strip of cloth in the ultimate catfight.

SHARON flies Abigail through the friendly skies that only two women can know . . . together.

HERMAN BERMAN submits to the point of Moira's passionate whip—and learns to love each luscious lash.

Merry old England gets positively precarious—when it meets these two birds of a fabulous feather.

Books by
Aston Cantwell

Double Delight
Tease For Two

Published by
WARNER BOOKS

Tease for Two

Aston Cantwell

WARNER BOOKS

A Warner Communications Company

For David Gale,
a source of lasting inspiration

Tease for Two

Chapter One

Abigail tilted the passenger seat back and made herself comfortable in its soft leather. She half closed her eyes and ran her hands down the front of her party costume, smoothing the white silk across the curves of her body. "I feel like doing something outrageous tonight," she said.

"Yeah?" Brad glanced at her from the driver's seat. "Like what?"

Abigail shifted her thighs restlessly. "Oh, I don't know. Like dropping ice cubes down some movie producer's pants, or exposing myself in public, or something." She giggled playfully.

Brad glanced at her again, then guided the Mercedes around the next curve with a series of nervous arm movements. "Uh, you said this was going to be a real exclusive party, Abigail. I mean, with real big names there. Like it won't be just another Hollywood show-biz thing. I mean with senators and oil corporation presidents and— I mean, you made it sound like this would be like the party of the year."

"I won't embarrass you, Brad." She spoke as if she were reassuring a small boy. She patted him on the leg. "You're so uptight, dear. Why don't you smoke a joint or something?"

"No. I don't want to screw up my perceptions in any way. See, for you this is no big deal, Abigail. But for me,

9

this party could be extremely important, as regards my career."

"Mmm-hmm." She let her head loll back against the headrest and stared idly out of the side window. Sunset had faded to a dim red line at the horizon. The evening sky was purple-black. As the car rounded the next corner on Mulholland Drive, the wide expanse of the valley came into view, spangled with a million lights.

Abigail squirmed in her seat, pulled up the voluminous skirts of her costume, and groped beneath her petticoats. She wriggled her hips and started easing her panties down her legs.

"What are you doing?" said Brad. He pushed the rumpled silk of Abigail's dress away from where it had engulfed the gearshift lever.

"Taking my underwear off," she told him. She slipped the skimpy, white lace panties down her legs and kicked them onto the floor. "There, that's better."

"What did you do that for?"

"So I can touch myself." She thrust her hand under her dress and the petticoats and probed with her fingertip between her thighs.

Brad shook his head. "You're unbelievable. Unbelievable! I mean, don't you ever get enough?"

"Not often." She smiled playfully. Her cute, freckled face, familiar to moviegoers all over America, relaxed into an expression of simple pleasure. She parted her lips and let out a slow sigh of satisfaction.

"You're distracting me from my driving, Abigail."

"Then, stop driving," she murmured. She glanced at him—a brief, meaningful look—then closed her eyes and continued masturbating.

Brad didn't say anything for a while. Then abruptly he hit the brakes and pulled the car to the side of the highway. He turned the wheel and shifted down to first gear. The Mercedes bumped off the road and onto the grassy shoulder overlooking the lights of Hollywood.

"You decided to give me a hand?" Abigail asked. "If

you'll excuse the pun." She smiled again and her face dimpled. She reached down and pressed the handle beside her seat. The seat reclined under her, all the way back.

Brad squirmed around and made as if to lie on top of her, but she quickly brought her hands up and held him away. "No, you'll wrinkle my gown," she told him.

He gestured helplessly. "Then, what—"

Abigail moved her hands to his shoulders. She started pushing him gently but firmly toward her crotch. "If you want to," she said, licking her lips with just the tip of her pink tongue. "You always make it feel so good, Brad."

He stared up at her as if tormented by her. He was a slim, handsome young man, his thick black hair a trifle long, his dark eyes very intense. She'd met him while making her most recent movie. He'd had a bit part as a restaurant waiter, in just one scene. Something about him had appealed to her. He'd taken his few lines so seriously, as if it were his big break in the movie business. He was so dedicated, so ambitious—so eager to please. Right away he'd latched on to her in the hope that she might help him with his career—if he satisfied her every whim.

And, Abigail thought to herself now, maybe she would help him. She enjoyed having him as her tame gigolo, hanging around her, courting her, doing errands for her, and making love to her whenever she wanted him to. After all, he was not only eager to please, he was good at it....

He ducked his head down between her thighs. She opened her legs wide and propped her heels on the dashboard. Brad wriggled down onto the floor and slid his hands up under her legs till he had grasped her by her ass. He lifted her hips up and held her crotch against his mouth. He started lapping her eagerly.

Abigail reached down and pulled Brad's face harder against her crotch. His tongue thrust into her vagina. He had such a long tongue, and it probed so deep! Abigail

11

gasped and wiggled her hips in delight. Brad stabbed his tongue in and out, in and out, at the same time massaged her labia with his lips. His fingers clenched under her ass.

Abigail sighed with pleasure. She couldn't think of any other man who had ever given her oral sex as well as Brad did. He dedicated himself to the task, and he went on, and on, and on. . . .

He moved his tongue from her vagina to her clitoris. He licked it fleetingly at first, sending little tingles through Abigail's lissome body. Then he licked it harder, in slow but persistent strokes. He kissed it, sucked on it, and rubbed his soft, moist lips up and down across it.

Abigail reached inside the bodice of her gown and slid her fingers over her breasts. She clutched herself and pinched her own nipples between finger and thumb. She closed her eyes and savored the waves of arousal rippling through her. She breathed in quick little gasps.

Brad's tongue licked her clitoris harder and faster. He sensed the tension building in her and he knew he could make her come in just a few minutes more. He sucked, he nibbled, his lips made wet noises, his breath was a hot caress.

Abigail tried to delay her orgasm so she could savor the sensations for as long as possible. She clenched her fists and willed herself not to come. She bit her lip. She tried not to think about what he was doing.

But Brad only tried harder to please her. His tongue wiggled her clitoris from side to side, flicking to and fro so fast she felt as if there were a vibrator pressed against her crotch. Abigail's head fell back, and she let out a long, slow moan. She whimpered. Her fingers groped for him and clutched at his hair. She arched her back and thrust her hips up. She was throbbing, and she was almost at the edge—

Though her eyes were closed, she suddenly realized there was a light shining on her face, making her eyelids turn red as if she were out in the sun. Abigail opened her eyes with a start, and winced. A powerful flashlight beamed in through the car's windshield.

"Brad!" she gasped. "Quick, Brad!"

But with his head buried between her legs, he seemed not to hear her. Either that, or he assumed she was crying out in passion. He went on licking her clit for all he was worth.

Abigail gulped and gasped. She floundered helplessly, dizzy with the waves of sex sensation. And still Brad licked her eagerly. Meanwhile, outside the car, the person holding the flashlight came around to the passenger window. Dazzled by the light, Abigail couldn't see who was behind it. Then she looked to the left and realized a police patrol car had parked alongside.

Abigail reached down and pushed frantically at Brad's face, trying to stop him from licking her. But he hunkered down, evaded her grasp, and went on doing it to her single-mindedly.

The cop rapped with his knuckles on Abigail's window.

In desperation Abigail quickly threw her skirt down over Brad's head. There was so much of the fabric it easily concealed him. With any luck the flashlight beaming in through the windshield would not betray his presence. The cop would just see Abigail lying back in her seat with her eyes closed.

She rolled down her window. "What is it?" she asked, trying to keep her voice casual.

"You're not allowed to stop here," said the cop. He clicked off his flashlight and she saw his face—middle-aged, stern, and unfriendly.

"I know," she said. "But I— I was tired, so I pulled over just for a minute and—"

"This your car, lady?"

"Yes. Yes, it is." Down beneath her skirt Brad had stopped licking her at last. Realizing that something had happened, he was now trying to pull himself free. Abigail quickly clenched her thighs and gripped his head between them. There was a muffled protest.

"Here," Abigail said quickly, opening the glove compartment. "Here's the registration."

The cop scrutinized it. "Abigail van Pelt?" He looked from the registration to her face. "Miss van Pelt, I'm sorry. I didn't recognize you." His voice suddenly became much more friendly. "In your gown there, you look like some kind of princess."

"That's right," Abigail agreed with a nervous laugh. "That's how I'm supposed to look. I'm going to a costume party, you see." Once again, beneath her dress, Brad tried to struggle up for air. Abigail crossed her legs under the silk. She locked her thighs more tightly around Brad's face and smoothed the dress down with a quick wave of her hand. She felt the side of her palm strike through the fabric at where she judged Brad's nose to be. Sure enough, there was a muffled yelp, and his struggles suddenly diminished.

"Well, Miss van Pelt," the cop was saying, handing back Abigail's registration, "I'm sorry, but you'll have to move your car. There's a cross street a little ways down the hill. If you need to stop and rest for a while, you can park there."

"All right, I'll do that," she told him with a genteel smile. "I'm sorry I troubled you, officer."

"No trouble. Drive carefully, now." And he turned and walked back to his own car.

Abigail quickly put the window up, then squirmed across to the driver's seat. She started the engine. "Don't get up!" she hissed at Brad. "Stay there on the floor, dummy!"

"What the fuck is going on?" he complained. "Jesus Christ, you hit me in the eye!"

"Are you deaf, or something?" she snapped at him. She put the Mercedes in gear and took it carefully back onto the highway. The cop pulled out around her. She gave him a wave and a smile, and watched as he took off down the hill. Cautiously she started after him. Her skin was still hot and tingling, her mouth was dry, and her pussy was soaking wet with Brad's saliva and her own juices. She squirmed uncomfortably. She'd been right on the edge of orgasm.

"I just want to know——" Brad began again.

"It was a cop with a flashlight," she snapped. "Didn't you hear him?"

"I couldn't hear anything with your legs pressed over my ears."

"Well, it was the Los Angeles police department, and neither one of us needs that kind of publicity. All right, you can get up now." She ran her fingers shakily through her long blond hair. "I'm sorry I snapped at you, Brad," she added in a gentler tone. "Jesus, talk about coitus interruptus! I'm so damned horny!"

He scrambled onto the passenger seat beside her and brushed at his clothes. "My costume's all messed up," he complained. He'd chosen to dress as a court jester for the costume party, and was clad in red and yellow, with little bells sewn around the cuffs of his pants. The bells jingled as he tried to brush off the dust and dirt.

"Yes, and meanwhile I'm leaking all over my gown," said Abigail. She drove with one hand, reached for some Kleenex, and tried to mop her crotch. But the touch of the tissues made her feel even more horny. "A fine mood I'm in for this party," she muttered, revving the engine and taking the car too fast around a curve.

Brad reached across tentatively. "I could touch you while you——"

"No, let's not try and start up all over again. That cop probably patrols along here, back and forth, all night. I'm not going to risk parking illegally again up here, and there's nowhere else we could do it." She sighed. "I guess I'll just have to stay horny—till after the party, anyway."

She didn't know how wrong she would turn out to be.

Chapter Two

"Cocaine, madam?"

The elderly English butler offered Abigail a silver tray. On it was a rather large, antique silver snuffbox, its lid open to reveal a couple ounces of sparkling white coke.

"Why, thank you, I don't mind if I do," said Abigail. She took one of the delicate little silver spoons laid out on the tray and used it to scoop up a sample, first to one nostril, then to the other. Was it bad etiquette, she wondered, not to straighten one's little finger while snorting coke? Dressed like a princess, she ought to act the part— not that anyone here would have noticed. It looked as if the party had already degenerated into a drugged and drunken shambles.

"Thank you," Abigail told the butler with a thin, regal smile. She hesitated, feeling the cocaine hitting her hard. She blinked, determined not to lose her poise. "Brad?" She turned to see if he wanted any.

"No. No, I'm keeping my head straight," he told her. "Your tiara's slipping to one side," he added.

"Well, can you deal with it for me?" She turned to face him, moving a little unsteadily on her feet.

Brad reached up and carefully repositioned the fake-gold tiara she was wearing. The nearness of him made her feel horny again. She was still wet inside from his attentions in the car. Impulsively she reached down, grabbed his crotch, and massaged it.

"Hey, cut that out!" he hissed at her, looking nervously to either side. "Later, all right?"

Abigail giggled. "I've never seen you so uptight," she told him, then turned and walked down some steps into the huge sunken living room. It was crowded with people in costumes of every description, rented from the movie supply houses of Hollywood: cowboy clothes, army uniforms, nurses, doctors, apes, clowns, bears, astronauts, cavemen, harlequins, priests, and demons all mingling together. Champagne and cocaine were circulating freely. Rock music was playing, and a few guests were dancing clumsily. Outside the giant windows that filled one wall of the room, people were frolicking in the swimming pool and fornicating on the lawn.

"There's Mr. Berman," said Brad eagerly. "Over in the corner by the videotape unit. We ought to go say hello to him, Abigail. I mean, it is his party, right?"

"Keep calm, Brad, dear. Yes, I'll introduce you." She took his hand and led him through the throng. Actually, Herman Berman, onetime porno movie king and men's magazine magnate, was hardly a friend of Abigail's. Years ago, when she'd been a struggling actress in need of quick money, she'd done some hardcore eight-millimeter loops for him on the quiet; her name had been on his invitation list ever since. These days, however, he was producing high-class movies and running a men's magazine that had become respectable enough to feature excerpts from Mailer's latest novel and articles by Gore Vidal.

Abigail knew that when Berman saw her it would probably remind him of his days as a sleazy-movie mogul, which wasn't what he wanted at all. Still, Brad needed the contacts, so Abigail strolled across the angle-deep beige carpet to the video projector in the corner showing scenes from Berman's new movie.

"Herman, dear," she exclaimed, catching hold of his arm. "What a delightful party."

It took him several seconds to focus on her face, and several more seconds before he figured out who she was. "Yeah, ah, Abby, a pleasure," he muttered, totally stoned. He was dressed in a monk's habit, as if to proclaim the fact that he was a sex merchant no more. His fat face was red and sweating.

"My companion, Brad Milford," Abigail said with a warm smile.

"I'm delighted to meet you, Mr. Berman," Brad said eagerly and earnestly, grabbing Berman's hand and shaking it. "I've been a fan of your work ever since your early movies. I mean the very early ones, like *Sex Crazed Susan*. You know, even in that early work I think it's possible to see the essence of your genius as a director. I realize the films were not critically respectable, but—"

Abigail exited discreetly, leaving Brad to gabble the monologue she realized he'd been rehearsing all day. Berman was cringing, an expression of horror on his face, but with Brad holding on to his hand, there wasn't much he could do.

"Abigail, dear!"

Abigail turned, hearing a voice that sounded deceptively like her own, except that it had more of an edge to it. "Why, Moira," she said, without too much enthusiasm. "I should have guessed you'd be here."

Moira was Abigail's twin sister, and also her manager. The two women looked identically beautiful, except that Moira kept her hair cut short and dyed a businesslike black. Her face also tended to look more aggressive and severe than Abigail's, reflecting the greed that was a driving force in her life.

The periodic feuds and fights between Moira and Abigail had become legendary in Hollywood. Knowing this, Abigail deliberately hugged Moira now, with a wide, happy smile, and kissed her warmly on the cheek. If there were any gossip columnists present, she didn't want to give them a chance to invent new rumors of discord between the two sisters.

"Love your costume, dear," Moira said, taking in Abigail's flowing gown of white silk, her royal blue sash, and her crown studded with fake gems.

"Oh, you too," Abigail said, looking in stunned disbelief at Moira's outfit—a skintight, laced-up black-leather bodysuit, a form-fitting dominatrix outfit that gripped her like a giant corset, revealing only the tops of her breasts, which were pushed up so high they seemed just a couple of inches below her chin. She was wearing boots with five-inch heels, and carried a coiled, braided leather whip.

"The nice thing about costume parties is that I can come as I am," Moira said with a strange look in her eye.

"Yes, er, of course," muttered Abigail in confusion. "But where's George?"

"Why, right here, darling." Moira jerked on a chrome-plated chain she held in her left hand. Abigail looked down and saw that Moira's assistant, George, was on his hands and knees on the floor, dressed up as a Saint Bernard dog. The chain was attached to a heavy leather collar around his neck.

"George, sit," said Moira. Obediently George sat on his haunches. "Now, give Abigail your paw." And George held out his fur-clad hand.

"Hi, George," Abigail said, shaking his paw and forcing a smile. "It must be hot as hell inside that thing," she said to Moira.

"Oh, it is," Moira answered with a dreamy, malicious look. "But he loves it, don't you, dear?" She jerked on the chain, and George made throttled noises and tugged futilely at the collar.

"Hmm. Yes. Well, see you around." Abigail turned and slid away as quickly as she could.

She walked outside. The night was warm and inviting. Guests were splashing around in the huge swimming pool, lit by underwater floodlights. Abigail was beginning to wish she hadn't worn such an expensive, elaborate costume; it would be good to strip it off and dive in the water. But she'd decided she had to wear something with class. Despite Brad's ideas about this party being an important social event, Abigail knew Berman's parties always degenerated to the level of a zoo. Sure, there were high-ranking oil executives and foreign diplomats here, but they were usually the ones who behaved worst of all, given a few snorts of coke and a couple glasses of champagne.

"Excuse me, madam."

The voice came from beside her shoulder. Abigail turned quickly and found one of the English waiters standing there. He held out something. "Lord Barrington asked that I convey this to you, madam."

Abigail saw it was a small card. She took it and squinted at the tiny script. His Royal Highness, Lord Barrington of Beauleigh. She looked back at the butler. "And where is this—this lord?" she asked with a smile.

"He awaits your pleasure under the elm tree, madam. May I present you to him?"

"Sure," said Abigail, thinking the guy was overacting, but she was enjoying the charade. She followed the servant across the lawn, into the shadows. "You're one of Herman Berman's waiters, aren't you?"

"No, madam. I am Lord Barrington's aide-de-camp."

"Oh really," said Abigail, detouring around a man and woman having passionate sex in the grass.

The servant led her to a bench beneath a large, old elm tree. "Lord Barrington, may I present Miss Abigail van Pelt," he said.

Abigail peered into the semidarkness. There was just enough illumination from the distant floodlights outside the mansion for her to make out a man in the costume of a king, complete with gold crown and velvet robes. He looked to be around thirty, with a wide, square jaw, long aristocratic nose, and an easy, relaxed air, despite his formal garb. He stood up, bowed to Abigail, took her hand, and kissed it. "I'm delighted to meet you," he said. He turned to the servant. "That will be all, Richardson."

"Very well, sir." The butler disappeared discreetly into the shadows.

"Is that a real English accent?" Abigail asked.

"Yes, it is, actually."

"I thought so. But you never know; in Hollywood, at a thing like this—so many goddamn actors. That's a neat costume you got."

"It's not bad, is it?" he agreed. "I saw you walk into the living room a few minutes ago," he went on. "It seemed natural, you and me, dressed as king and queen . . ."

"Yeah. I, ah, figured that much." She looked at his face again and decided she liked what she saw. "That's a nice little routine, with your manservant and all. Is he a pal of yours or something?"

"That's right."

"Kind of an elaborate way to pick up girls, isn't it?"

He straightened his posture and looked down at her with mock severity. "One has to preserve a sense of decorum, madam. Surely, you agree?"

Abigail giggled. She felt high and free, and she remembered telling Brad, in the car, that she felt like doing something outrageous. "I've never been too big on decorum, myself. So anyway, Lord Barrington, how's it going? You done any movies over here? What sort of roles do you play? Would I have seen you in anything?"

"My God, I've only been in Los Angeles for a few days. And films aren't really my, ah, forté."

Abigail nodded. "I see. You prefer the stage, huh? I envy you the theatrical work you can get over in your country."

"Well, the theater is one of our greatest traditions, it's true." He gestured to the bench under the tree. "Shall we sit down?"

"Why not?" She joined him there. "So you're on a visit, or what?"

"Just a visit," he agreed. "Incidentally, I must tell you, I've seen all your films. Always wanted to meet you, miss— Abigail?"

She reached up and took off her tiara. "Yeah, let's keep this informal. I mean, it's always fun to act a part, but kind of a drag to keep it up all night."

"Oh, I agree. Absolutely." He reached up and took off his crown, and laid it beside hers. "That's better," he said. "That thing was giving me a headache."

She reached up and ruffled his hair where the crown had flattened it. He had thick, untidy hair, and it gleamed gold in the lights from the house. He was handsome, and there was something about him she liked. Maybe just the accent. It made him sound so respectable, so high class, and yet she sensed he could be a rogue too. "So you're heading back to the old country soon?" she asked, trying to keep her voice casual.

He nodded. He was watching her closely.

It's ideal, Abigail thought to herself. She could have a quick fling with him, here, and even if he developed a crush on her, he'd be out of the country within days. No messy involvements, and no conflict with Brad, who tended to get so damned jealous and possessive.

Abigail leaned back against the tree. She smoothed down her gown and arched her back, pushing her breasts up. She tossed her blond hair away from her face and looked at the Englishman with her head to one side. She gave him a sly smile. "So why'd you invite me out here?" she asked softly. "Just wanted to talk?"

He paused a moment, still studying her. He seemed half serious, half amused. "Perhaps," he said.

"You British, always so reserved," said Abigail, giddy from the champagne, bold with the cocaine, and still horny from the unfinished scene with Brad in her Mercedes. "You're in Los Angeles now." She sat forward, then reached out and took his face between her hands. She pressed her mouth hard against his.

He responded uncertainly at first, then with passion.

23

His lips parted. His hands took hold of her shoulders.

Abigail pulled back after just a moment. "That's better," she said with a smile.

"You American women, so forthright," he told her quietly.

"You're complaining?"

He shook his head. "Never." He stood up, stooped and gathered her in his arms, and lifted her. Quickly then, he carried her deeper into the shadows.

Chapter Three

He carried her to a secluded corner where a cluster of pine trees stood close together. Their fragrance was rich in the night air. He lowered her to the ground, which was carpeted in dry pine needles. He sat beside her, took her face between his hands, and kissed her.

It was a slow, tentative kiss, gentle at first, his lips brushing across hers, then touching and pressing harder. His hand slid down and cupped her breast. He felt her nipple standing up tight and hard beneath the silk, and he pinched it gently between his finger and thumb. His other hand went behind her back, pressing her body against his. Then he caressed her neck, his fingers stroking her soft, soft skin.

He circled her with his arms and looked down at her as if he were savoring her.

She reached up and stroked his face. "There's something...gentlemanly about you," she said. "The way you are with me."

"Is that good or bad?"

"Good. Because you've got a sense of humor too." She started fumbling with the royal uniform he was wearing under his velvet robes. "How the hell does this thing come undone?"

"Lots of metal buttons," he told her. "Here, let me. What about your dress? Won't it get dirty on the ground?"

"I don't care," she told him. "I'll have it cleaned before I return it." She reached behind her neck and unfastened the hooks and the zipper. Then she pulled the dress up and over her head and threw it aside in a rustle of silk and satin. She stood up then, and slid out of her petticoats.

"Not wearing panties?" he said.

Abigail realized they were still back in the car, where she'd kicked them off earlier. She reached behind her, unhooked her bra, and slid out of it. "Now I'm not wearing a bra either," she told him. She stood naked, enjoying the way he watched her. The smooth curves of her body were outlined by moonlight filtering down between the pines. Her long, tousled hair shimmered. She stretched and arched her back, then caressed her own breasts. She walked toward him.

"No, don't sit down," he told her. "Stand there a moment longer." He finished stripping off the last of his clothes, then kneeled in front of her. He kissed her belly, and she felt the smooth dry skin of his cheek against her. Then he ran the tip of his tongue lower, through her pubic hair. His hands circled around behind her ass. He buried his head between her thighs and drew her against him. His tongue crept down into her cleft. Abigail gasped and shivered when he found her clitoris. She was still so hot and horny from the scene with Brad in the car she felt she could come almost within seconds.

He ran his tongue lightly to and fro across her clitoris. He licked her insistently, till Abigail felt all her muscles clench. Her knees trembled, and she had to steady herself by reaching down and holding on to his shoulders. But then, just as she thought she was about to climax, he drew back.

She took a deep, shuddering breath. The sensations died down a little—but only a little. She was still on the edge of orgasm. He kissed the insides of her thighs and nibbled the soft, tender skin there. He licked around her labia, he

26

kissed her clitoris, and then he started licking it again.

Standing in front of him, Abigail closed her eyes. She quivered at his touch and gave an involuntary cry. She slid her fingers into his hair and urged him to lick her harder. She was once again coming close, so close to a climax—

And again he drew back, leaving her on the brink. She gasped. "Don't stop!"

"But I've hardly begun," he murmured to her. He scrambled quickly to his feet and stood naked in front of her. He grabbed her and pulled her body against his. His skin felt warm, and his flesh was firmly muscled. He smelled faintly of cologne. He kissed her hard, and Abigail felt as if she were melting in his grip. His cock stood out very large and hard, nudging between her legs. The pressure of it made the yearning ache inside her grow still more insistent.

He reached down and rubbed his fingertip across her clitoris, ever so lightly. He watched her face as he touched her. She clutched at him. Her breath came in erratic little gasps. He played with her, savoring her arousal. She wanted to tell him to stop teasing her and let her come, but somehow he had taken command of the lovemaking, and she couldn't put the words together. She felt helpless as he caressed her clitoris and watched her tremble with desire for him.

He stopped touching her and moved his hand up her body, trailing his fingernails across her flesh, not hard enough to hurt but hard enough to make her flinch. He caressed her high, firm breasts, lightly at first, then with sudden passion. He dug his fingers into the soft flesh. He moved his other hand behind her neck and kissed her again, holding her head so that she couldn't pull away.

Then he pushed her down onto the ground. He grabbed her by the shoulders and kissed her some more. His tongue thrust into her mouth. He rolled on top of her. She opened her legs instinctively and felt his cock straining against her labia. She reached down to put it inside her.

He caught her wrist and pulled her hand away. He kept hold of her wrist and forced it down on the ground above her head. He took her other wrist and held that beside the first. He let her feel the weight of his body. He had her pinned so she couldn't move.

She closed her eyes and turned her face to one side, feeling just a little scared of him. He was so deliberate and forceful, and somehow she seemed to have lost the ability to resist—not that she wanted to, but it was strange to feel that she no longer even knew how to resist.

Slowly and deliberately he took hold of his cock with his free hand and rubbed the head of it up and down between her labia. She cried out. She wrapped her legs around him, urging him into her.

He allowed just the first inch of his cock inside her. He paused then, and rocked very slightly to and fro.

Abigail squirmed under him. She tried to thrust her hips up against him.

He pushed another inch into her. And then an inch more. His cock was very wide, and she felt as if he was filling her whole body. She bit her lip and whimpered.

And then he pushed in suddenly, all the way. She screamed and clung to him. He ground his hips against her. He wrapped both arms around her and held her so she couldn't move. He started fucking her in very slow, hard strokes.

Abigail writhed under him, rubbing her body against his. She felt the hairs of his chest against her nipples, his breath upon her face, and the shape of the muscles in his belly where it touched hers. All her senses were heightened. She gasped and clung close. He pushed deep, deep into her. He ground against her, as if he knew instinctively exactly how to rub himself against her clitoris. She was adrift in a cascade of sensations. She felt herself losing

28

all control. The feelings grew and grew—and then, at last, she climaxed.

It seemed to go on and on. She felt him reach down and press his finger against her clitoris, prolonging her orgasm. He held his cock deep inside her and hugged her body against his as she shook with the spasms.

Finally she relaxed, gasping for breath.

He kissed her, gently now. Then he resumed fucking her. He increased his speed and raised himself over her till he held himself above her with his arms stretched out straight. He watched her as he fucked her in a relentless rhythm. She bit her lip and trembled at the force of his thrusts. In the faint moonlight she saw sweat break out on his forehead. His breathing became labored. He groaned and clenched his teeth. His cock seemed to swell up even larger than before.

Then he came. He plunged deep and held himself there so that she could feel his cock jerking inside her. He reached down and grabbed one of her breasts and held it as he came. Then he cupped her chin in his hand, bent his head, and kissed her tenderly.

When his orgasm was over, he fell down onto her, clutching her against him, and rolled onto his side, pulling her with him and still keeping himself inside her. He stroked his fingertip down her cheek, then caressed her face. He kissed her forehead. Together, they lay in silence for a few moments, both of them enjoying the afterglow.

"You're even more beautiful in real life than in your films," he said quietly.

Abigail smiled uncertainly. Sex had left her feeling sated, but confused and dizzy too. She'd expected a quick, brief coupling in the grass, not this intense, strangely emotional experience. She closed her eyes and tried to think about Brad, to bring herself back to reality and maybe even make herself feel a little guilty. But lying there with her eyes closed, she was still totally conscious of the Englishman holding her against him.

She felt his cock wtihdraw from her. Without knowing exactly what she was doing or why, she squirmed down and kissed his thighs, then licked his semen and her own juices from the head of his penis.

"You want to make love some more?" he asked her.

"No. No, I . . . just wanted to taste you."

She drew back suddenly, then stood up. "Jesus Christ, I don't even know your name. What did it say on that phony calling card? Lord something?"

"Barrington." He lay on the carpet of pine needles, watching her as she paced to and fro.

"Yeah. Lord Barrington. So who are you really?"

"Barrington's my real name. James Barrington."

"Oh. James. How British." She stopped and studied him for a moment. Then she shook her head as if trying to wake herself out of a dream. She turned deliberately away from him. She put her hands on her hips. "Well, I guess we should get back to the party."

He stood up quickly and reached to embrace her. At first she tried to resist, then reluctantly let him hold her.

"What's wrong?" he asked.

"Nothing's wrong." She avoided his eyes.

"I felt very close to you just now," he told her. "And you seemed to feel the same way."

Abigail hesitated. "Well . . . that's true." She drew a deep breath. "Look, this is all kind of intense. I mean, I just met you, and I didn't expect—"

"You want it to be casual," he said. He shrugged. "As you wish, Miss van Pelt." He opened his arms and released her. Suddenly he seemed cold and distant and reserved, and despite herself, she felt abandoned.

She stood and watched him as he picked up his clothes and started putting them on. "That's some costume you got there, Lord Barrington," she said, determined not to show any of her true feelings.

"It's not a costume," he told her as he fastened the gold buttons of the tunic.

"What's that supposed to mean?" she said.

"I mean this is my dress uniform. It's real."

A slow suspicion began to form in her mind. "Are you trying to tell me—"

He looked at her matter-of-factly. "I'm a bona-fide aristocrat, Miss van Pelt. In fact I'm a distant relation in the British Royal Family. A second cousin of the Duke of Edinburgh. Technically, I believe I'm something like 275th in line of succession to the throne. But the exact number changes as various people in between die off or have children."

"But you said you were an actor!"

He shook his head. "No, you said that. Since that seemed to be what you wished to believe, I decided not to disabuse you."

"Jesus Christ," said Abigail. "So what're you doing here at Berman's party?"

He shrugged. "I'm on diplomatic business. Escorting two Saudi Arabian sheiks. They wanted to see a decadent Hollywood party, so I had no choice but to accompany them. Sooner or later I suppose Richardson and I will have to find them, and sober them up and take them back to their wives in the Beverly Wilshire Hotel." He ran his fingers through his hair, straightened his uniform, then put on his velvet robe. "I only brought this stuff along for an official ceremony tomorrow," he went on. "But when I learned this was a costume party, it seemed appropriate. Also, quite frankly, I was pleased to save a little money by not having to rent a costume. The royal budget isn't as big as it used to be, you know."

"I see," Abigail said blankly. She realized she was staring at him.

He walked over and kissed her perfunctorily on the forehead. "I say, aren't you going to get dressed?"

She closed her eyes a moment. She felt disoriented. "That's not how you kissed me before," she murmured.

"No. But you did say you wanted this to be a casual thing, didn't you?"

She didn't answer.

"So you'd better put on your . . . your princess outfit," he said with a sardonic smile. "And then we can go back to the party."

Chapter Four

Abigail walked back to the house with Lord James Barrington. They stopped along the way to pick up her tiara and his gold crown from the bench where they'd left them.

"This thing is real, too?" she asked, taking the crown from him for a moment and feeling how heavy it was. "The jewels as well?"

He shrugged. "Its exact origins aren't definite. I believe it was Dutch; it came to Britain by some roundabout fashion two hundred or so years ago, and was donated to the family legacy. The rubies, there, are the only really precious stones."

"But it must be worth a fortune. You shouldn't leave it lying around out here."

As he took it from her, his fingers touched hers for a moment, making sharp, brief physical contact.

"I suppose you'd call me a romantic, Abigail. When a woman truly excites my interest—" He shrugged. "I tend to forget little matters such as whether I've left the family jewels in safe keeping. Anyway, the guests here are too drunk and too rich to go around stealing heirlooms." He turned and strolled on toward the house.

Abigail followed him. "I can be a romantic myself, once in a while," she said.

"When you're not being . . . casual?" He smiled as if he were mocking her.

She reached out and grabbed his arm. "Stop a minute." She paused, not sure what she really wanted to say. "My . . . boyfriend . . . is in the house somewhere. I'll have to find him. But look, are you going to have any free time in the next couple of days? Before you head back to . . . to jolly old England?" She tried to make it sound flippant, but the words came out plaintive.

"Let's meet tomorrow," he said. His voice was quiet, but a deep, rich baritone. He looked at her steadily, as if he understood her perfectly. "Quite possibly, Abigail, this is one of those brief encounters that one should not try to repeat. But if we don't try, we will never know for certain, will we?"

Abigail laughed unsteadily. "That's quite a line you have, Lord Barrington."

He took her face between his hands and kissed her slowly and thoroughly on the mouth. Then he straightened up and looked at her for a moment. Now that they were closer to the lights of the house, she could see him more clearly. He was very tall, easily over six feet, and he stood with a regal posture—a straight back, his chin held high— that made him seem even taller. There was pride in his face and confidence, but kindness and humor besides.

"Suppose we meet in the Polo Lounge of the Beverly Wilshire, tomorrow at four," he went on. "Does that sound reasonable?"

"It sounds crazy, but I guess I'll be there."

"One thing, though," he cautioned her, catching her arm. "We do have to be rather discreet. As one of Her Majesty's retinue, I'm not supposed to indulge in, ah, this kind of thing, while engaged in affairs of state."

"Gotcha," said Abigail, and laughed nervously. "You're so British, it's like watching a movie." Now that she'd made the date with him, she didn't feel so uptight any more. She kissed him quickly on the cheek. "See you tomorrow." She winked. And then she ran back toward the house, her white gown rippling behind her in the wind.

She reached the swimming pool and straightaway saw Brad. He was standing in front of some drunken couples sitting on deck chairs.

"All right, now this is my Bogart imitation," he was saying. He cleared his throat and gestured dramatically. "Here'sh lookin' at you, kid. . . ."

"Hey, Brad," Abigail interrupted, grabbing him by the shoulder.

"Not now," he complained, turning and frowning at her. He lowered his voice. "Don't you understand, Abigail, this could be—"

"A big break for you, sure," she said wearily.

"Can you do Cagney?" asked a dumb blond sitting beside a fat producer who had passed out, his head on her shoulder and his hand inside her bikini top.

"Sure," said Brad. "See, I'm a versatile kind of a guy; I can handle almost any kind of a role. Now Jimmy Cagney . . ."

Abigail wrinkled her nose in disgust at the way Brad was toadying to his audience of degenerates. She turned and walked to the swimming pool.

It was full of paper plates and plastic glasses, and couples making out. Some of them were still half-dressed. Their sodden clothes clung to their bloated flesh. Abigail grimaced. She walked on, around the side of the house, to the giant whirlpool bath that Berman had installed there and landscaped to look like a grotto. Colored spotlights were hidden among the rocks and succulent plants. The lights played on the naked bodies of people frolicking in the churning water.

There were half a dozen men in the bath, and a single woman going from one to the next. Abigail heard shouts and squeals and drunken laughter. She squinted in the dim light and realized that it was her twin sister, Moira, in the water.

"Abigail?" a man's voice came from beside her.

Abigail turned quickly. "Who's that?"

"It's George. You know, Moira's secretary."

She saw him then, half-hidden behind some ornamental bushes. He was still dressed in his dog costume, though the Saint Bernard head had been removed.

"What are you doing back there?" she asked him.

"Moira tied me up." He gestured to the chain that went from his collar to a nearby tree. "I complained that I was getting too hot inside this thing, so she said she'd punish me for complaining by locking me up, here, and making me watch her have sex with all those other men."

Abigail examined the chain. It was secured around the tree with a padlock; there was no way she could release George. "My sister is a sick bitch," she muttered.

"I hate her," said George. He sounded drunk. "She beats me, she humiliates me, she orders me around all the time. . . ."

"So, how come you haven't walked out on her, after all these months?"

"I need her," he mumbled. "I guess, I— I need the way she treats me. I'm so hopeless, I need the discipline. She's so sexy, she turns me on so much, and she does such terrible things to me."

"Enough," said Abigail. She put her hands over her ears. "More than enough." She turned away from George and his neurotic monologue. She took a last look at the whirlpool and saw Moira lying on her back in the water. One man was holding her by her waist. Another was pushing his cock into her mouth. A third was fucking her clumsily, standing between her legs. Abigail recognized the guys: two studio vice-presidents and one famous scriptwriter. True to form, Moira was making it only with men who were useful business contacts.

Abigail walked quickly back to where Brad was still entertaining his small audience of drugged and drunken movie parasites.

"I know you'll recognize this one," he was saying. "This is a TV personality who—"

"Stop it," she snapped at him.

He looked at her, confused by her sharp tone. "What's the matter?"

"You're making a fool of yourself. None of these dummies is anyone important, and none of them gives a shit. They think you're a joke. Come on." She grabbed his wrist and dragged him after her, into the house.

"But Abigail—"

"No one respects you if you don't respect yourself." She hauled him into the living room. The music was playing much louder now. Most people who were still able to stand were dancing. Abigail grabbed two glasses of champagne from a passing waiter and thrust one at Brad. "Drink this, and stop acting like an asshole."

He winced as if she'd hit him. Reluctantly he took the glass from her. "You don't think I was making a good impression out there? You know some of my imitations—"

"For Christ's sake, Brad!" She didn't know why he suddenly seemed so useless, so pathetic, but it was driving her crazy. "Listen to me! You want auditions, I'll get you auditions. You want contacts, I'll make them for you. But not here. The only kind of contact you're going to make here is if you want to peddle your ass to some faggot casting director. You want that?"

He shook his head.

"Then, drink your champagne and dance with me." That way, she realized, she'd perhaps be able to forget about Lord James Barrington. Drive the memory of him out of her head for the rest of the evening. She swallowed her own champagne in a single gulp, then grabbed another two glasses.

She forced three drinks in succession down Brad's throat. She made him dance with her. She danced wildly, getting lost inside the music. Then someone played a quieter tune, and she grabbed hold of Brad and moved slowly with him, pressing her body against him.

She ran her fingers through his hair and ruffled it. Then

she held him by his hair and kissed him hard on the mouth. "We've got unfinished business," she told him. Her voice was slurred now, from the booze.

"What do you mean?" There was a dazed look in his eyes.

"You know what I mean." She hustled him over to one corner of the huge living room. She slumped down with him on a big pillow-couch. She kissed him again and pushed her tongue into his mouth.

He pulled away from her. "Not here," he gasped.

"Yes, here. Why the hell not. Eat me, Brad. I want you to eat me, right now." She started pulling her dress up.

"But—"

"Jesus Christ, no one will notice. Didn't you see the people outside in the pool? Out there, or in here, what's the difference?" She hiked up her petticoats, grabbed his head, and pushed it down between her thighs. "Come on, Brad. I need it. I really need it."

Reluctantly he bent his head and began licking her pussy. Then he paused and looked up, embarrassed that someone might be watching. But the people dancing paid no attention at all A waiter, walking past, merely offered Abigail some more champagne. His face was expressionless.

Abigail took a glass and lay back comfortably in the pillows. She spread her legs wider and pushed her hips out toward Brad. He squirmed around and got down on the floor on his knees. Abigail moved her ass to the edge of the couch. Brad bowed his head and continued licking her clit, giving it all his attention now.

Abigail felt some of the tension seeping out of her muscles. She sipped her champagne and straightened her dress, feeling every inch the princess with her humble servant Brad, in his ridiculous court jester costume, on his knees before her. His agile tongue lapped at the mouth of her vagina, then moved back to her clitoris and licked and worried at it insistently. Abigail felt waves of warmth spreading through her. Her breathing quickened.

She knew she was going to come very quickly, so she tilted the champagne glass and swallowed it all down. She jerked her hips in counterpoint to the quick, eager movements of Brad's tongue. The tingling warm feelings built and built. Abigail arched her back and tensed, almost at her climax.

From where she was lying on the couch, she had a clear view through the big windows out to the swimming pool. Some people were walking past—two Arabs in turbans, and then a man in formal wear. In her state of drunken arousal, Abigail suddenly realized the man was James Barrington's aide-de-camp, Richardson. And then Barrington himself was walking past, saying something to the Arabs, oblivious to what was happening just the other side of the windows in the living room.

Abigail clenched her teeth. The wave of sensations reached its peak. She felt a strange twist of anger; she suddenly threw her champagne glass as the orgasm took hold of her.

The glass shattered against the wall, but the sound of breaking glass was lost in the loud music. James Barrington walked on past the windows and disappeared from view.

Abigail closed her eyes and lay limply on the cushions, breathing hard. She felt Brad get up from between her legs and lie beside her. He pulled her dress down to cover her nakedness.

"You all right?" she heard him ask.

"Yes, I'm fine, she said, feeling terrible. She suddenly hated herself for using him. She'd been treating him not so differently from the way her sister treated George: as a sex-servant.

"You, uh . . . tasted different," said Brad.

"Oh?" Abigail pretended surprise, but she knew why. She hadn't douched after James Barrington's lovemaking with her. Brad had tasted Lord Barrington's semen.

Abigail suddenly turned and hugged Brad against her. "It's not your fault," she muttered.

"What's not my fault? You know, you're in a weird mood, Abigail. What happened?"

"Nothing. Will you take me home now, Brad? I'm too drunk to drive."

"Sure," he said, ever agreeable, ever eager to please.

He helped her stand up, and together they went outside to the graveled parking lot, full of Rolls-Royces and Porches and Mercedes.

Abigail glanced around, thinking she might catch another glimpse of James Barrington and his Saudi Arabian sheiks. But the parking lot was empty; Lord Barrington had already left.

Chapter Five

Meanwhile Abigail's twin sister Moira was drying herself after her sex frolics with the men in the pool. "Did you enjoy that, George?" she asked her captive secretary/sex-slave as she toweled her voluptuous body in front of him. "Did you like watching those men fuck me? Hmm?"

"No," George answered sullenly, still chained to the tree.

"But you always enjoy looking at my naked body," Moira teased, rubbing her hands over her curvy flesh and stepping closer to George—but not quite close enough for him to be able to touch her. "Don't you think I look beautiful?"

"Yes," said George, his voice barely audible.

Moira picked up her black-leather outfit and started putting it on. It was a tight fit, and she had to wiggle and wriggle to get into it. Despite himself, George watched every movement with obvious yearning.

"Well, George," she went on, "it seems to me you must've been jealous. Is that what was bothering you?"

George didn't answer.

Moira stepped closer to him. She gave him three little slaps on the cheek. "I asked you a question, darling," she said in a menacing voice.

"Yes . . . I was jealous," he mumbled.

"Tut, tut, tut," said Moira, stepping back from him. "You know you have no right at all to get jealous." She finished lacing up her leather costume. She put her boots on, then stood with her hands on her hips. "I think I'll have to punish you, George, dear."

His eyes widened in dismay. "Not here, Moira! Someone could see us!"

"Well, what if they do? Everyone's in costume, and most of them are drugged or stoned out of their minds. No one will pay any attention to our little game. It'll look like part of the show." Her eyes were bright. She licked her lips. Her teeth gleamed white in the semidarkness. "Come along, George. Do as I tell you. Pull down your pants."

"Oh, no, Moira! Please!" His voice was a pathetic whine—but of course the scene was beginning to turn him on despite his dread of it. To be spanked in public by his mistress! To be singled out for this special treatment! It was not only a punishment; in some strange way it was also an honor.

"Come on, you great big baby." She grabbed his doggie costume, found the zipper, and yanked his pants down around his ankles. "I'm so glad I told you not to put on any underwear, George," she added, half to herself, as she reached out and fondled his semi-erect penis. Then she held it in her fist and squeezed gently. She felt his cock getting hot and harder in her grip.

"Please, Moria!" he gasped, and tried to pull her arm away. But his hands were trapped inside the paws of his doggie outfit and he couldn't get a hold of her.

"Bend down!" she snapped at him suddenly.

Despite himself, George did as she said. He turned toward the tree she had chained him to, and bent forward and presented his bare ass to her.

"You will not be jealous!" Moira exclaimed. She brought her leather-gloved hand down on his bottom as hard as she could. It made a satisfying low-pitched thwacking sound.

"I will not be jealous, Mistress Moira," George repeated after her in a quavering voice.

"You will not bother me with any more of your tiresome whining and complaints!" Moira spanked him again, and then again. "I can do whatever I like with my body, without any criticism from you!" And she gave him one last smack. The force of it made him stagger, and the cheeks of his ass turned a shade of pink that was visible even in the dim light.

"That's better," Moira said, with a satisfied smirk. "Turn around, now."

George obeyed. His cock stood out very long and large, testifying to his having gotten off on the spanking, in his own way, just as much as Moira had.

"I suppose you're feeling horny now," she said, tickling his balls and stroking his penis. She licked her finger and rubbed it up and down the rigid shaft. "Do you want to fuck me, George, the way you saw those men fucking me in the pool?"

He was breathing heavily. "Yes, Mistress Moira."

"Well, I'm not going to let you. So there! Pull your pants up."

"Oh, but—"

"Do as I say!" she snapped at him. She unhooked a bunch of keys that dangled at her hip and unlocked the padlock securing George's chain to the tree. "Come along, doggie," she told him. "I'm going to take you for a little walk. Maybe . . . just maybe . . . if you're a very, very good little dog, I'll play with you . . . later on. But only if you're good."

George pulled his furry doggie-pants back up around his waist. The shape of his cock made a bulge at the crotch. He meekly followed Moira as she led him back toward the house.

A shadowy figure blocked the path. "Abigail?" said a voice.

Moira stopped. "I'm not Abigail, I'm Moira. Who are you?"

The figure shambled into the light. It was Herman Berman. His monk's habit was askew, and leaves and dry grass were sticking to it. His hair was disheveled and his face was red. He staggered drunkenly. He was holding his crotch with one hand. "Abigail," he mumbled again.

"No, no, Mr. Berman," Moira said with irritation. "I'm not Abigail. I'm her twin sister, Moira. I don't think you and I have ever met."

Berman slumped against a nearby tree. His eyes were on Moira's costume, and the way it cupped her plump breasts. "Saw you . . . saw you spanking your . . . friend," Berman muttered. He took his hand away from his crotch and flung his arm around the tree as if he were afraid of the ground shifting under his feet. Moira looked down and noticed that Berman had a huge erection under his clothes.

"You know, I trust you," Berman went on. "I mean, Abigail, we both got a past to live down, ain't that right?"

This time Moira didn't bother to correct him. If Herman Berman and her sister Abigail had some secrets to hide, Moira wanted to know about them. It could be useful, after all. Moira always had trouble keeping Abigail under control, and as for Berman, he was stinking rich and he produced respectable movies these days.

Moira stepped close to the drunk. She put her arm around his shoulders. "You liked what I was doing to George, over there?" she cooed into his ear.

"Mmm-hmm. C'mon, Abigail," he said. "Come upstairs to the private party. I trust you to keep a secret." He paused a moment and squinted at her. "What happened to your blond hair? Thought you had blond hair."

"Oh, this is just a wig," Moira said quickly.

"A wig?" Berman frowned. "You always had blond

hair. Looked beautiful. Don't know why you want to wear that black wig."

"I wear black when I punish naughty boys," said Moira. She studied Berman a moment and realized how she should deal with him. "But really, Herman, I'm surprised at you, asking such personal questions about my appearance." She licked her lips. "That's very disrespectful, you know. I do believe someone ought to teach you some manners. Teach you a lesson, in fact." She reached down and rubbed his bottom playfully.

Berman closed his eyes a moment. He swallowed hard. "Come on upstairs," he said, and lurched away along the path toward his mansion.

Moira and George followed Herman Berman into his mansion and across the vast entrance hall. It was styled like a medieval castle, with black and white flagstones on the floor, oak paneling and ornate carved woodwork, a giant chandelier laden with dozens of flickering candles, and heraldic banners hanging from the timbered ceiling thirty feet above. Berman staggered toward the staircase, picking his way over the prostrate bodies of guests, some of them drugged or drunk into unconsciousness, others half-naked and groping, or fucking each other.

"Bunch of bums!" Berman growled, stepping around a fat middle-aged man dressed as a cowboy, trying incompetently to take the bra off a young woman dressed as a nurse. Her eyes were shut and her mouth lolled open.

"Wilkins!" Berman shouted. "Wilkins, where the hell are you!" He took a deep breath and bellowed even louder. "Wilkins!"

One of the elderly British butlers hurried in from an adjoining room. "Yes, Mr. Berman?"

"Throw these bums out." Berman gestured at the bodies on the floor. "Anyone who can't stand up on his own two feet, throw 'em out into the parking lot. Let 'em sober up out there. I won't abide people who can't hold their liquor."

"Yes, Mr. Berman. I'll go and get some help."

"You do that. Come on, Abigail. Upstairs." He led Moira and George to the creaking oak staircase.

He paused halfway up, breathing heavily. His face had suddenly turned pale. "I sometimes have a little trouble at this point," he muttered. "Maybe it's the altitude." He turned on his heel and staggered to a giant rubber plant growing in a metal tub that stood in an alcove off the staircase. He stooped and vomited into the tub.

Berman straightened up and wiped his mouth on the sleeve of his monk's habit. He blinked. His face gradually recovered its bright red complexion. "That's better," he muttered. " 'Scuse me," he added to Moira. "Must've been something I ate. He climbed the rest of the staircase, reached the top, and paused to look down into the entrance hall, where his servants were dragging out the unconscious guests. "That's right, throw the bums out!" he shouted, waving his fist.

Then he led the way along a corridor, past imitation antique doors with wrought-iron hinges, and into a book-lined study.

He waited for Moira to enter the room, leading George after her in his doggie costume. Then Berman carefully closed the door of the study, and locked it. He went to one of the bookcases and pressed a concealed button. He leaned against the shelves and they swung inward with a gentle creaking noise.

"A secret, Abigail, all right?" He grinned and winked at her. "Come on, honey. This way to the private party. In here."

"Moira," George whispered to her. "Moira, I don't think we should—"

She turned on him. "I don't want to hear another word out of you!" she hissed. She jerked at the chain attached to his collar. "You'll follow me and keep quiet. Berman's a big shot movie producer these days, don't you understand that? He can be extremely useful to us. This is business, George, business. And you know how I deal with people, darling, when they interfere in my business affairs." She glared at him.

He cringed from her voice. "Yes, Moira."

"Now, follow me and do as you're told," she snapped, and led him through the secret doorway out of the study.

Chapter Six

Berman led the way down some stone steps and into a big room lit by dimly flickering neon candles. The floor and walls were of dark gray stone. The ceiling was lost in shadow.

Various devices made of rough-hewn oak and hammered wrought iron were standing around the edges of the room. There was a rack, an iron maiden, a bed of nails, and a rare implement that Moira recognized as St. Paul's Fingers—one of the most painful torture devices ever invented. There were shackles on the wall, trestles and iron rings set into the floor, and a wide assortment of whips, lashes, paddles, and canes standing in one corner, next to a large selection of dildos, gags, hoods, and leather restraints.

"Why," Moira exclaimed, clapping her hands together in delight, "this is the most wonderful dungeon I've ever seen!"

"I thought you'd like it, Abigail," Berman said, taking off his monk costume. "You see, honey, we have a lot of naughty boys up here visiting, tonight. I was just trying to find my dominary—domatry—" He took a deep breath. "My dominatrix, but I think she left the party already. Then I saw you." He shed the last of his costume. Under it, he was wearing white latex diapers. "You don't mind, do you," he went on, his voice rising in a pitch to a childish whine, "if I ask you to spank us naughty boys over here?"

"Why, of course," said Moira. "I can see you certainly deserve it. You've obviously been very, very bad indeed. You'd better introduce me to your friends." She turned to George. "Wait there," she said sternly.

Herman Berman, onetime prince of porn turned respectable movie producer and magazine publisher, led Moira to a lower level in the center of the dungeon—a wide, shallow pit lined with plastic straw. Five fat figures were sitting there, all of them middle-aged men, and all of them wearing baby clothes. Three of them were, in addition, wearing black leather masks, evidently out of fear of being recognized. The other two shamefacedly averted their eyes from Moira.

Herman Berman got down into the pit and slumped to his knees in the straw. "This is Johnny," he said, pointing to the first man. "And this is Billy, and Tommy, and Sammy, and Danny. And I'm Hermie. I was very bad today. I peed in my pants." He looked down at his latex diapers.

"I stole some candy," said Johnny.

"I called a lady a bad name," said Billy.

"I wet my bed last night," said Tommy.

"I spat out some of my din-dins," said Sammy.

"And I wouldn't eat my vegetables," said Danny.

"You see, Mithreth Abigail," Herman went on in a baby-voice, and with a lisp, "we thix naughty boyth play a little game here. We path thith rattle from hand to hand," he showed her a baby's rattle, "and when the music . . . the muthic stopth, the one holding the rattle gets hit."

"How do I turn on the music?" Moira asked.

"Your friend can thwitch it on. On the wall there. If you don't mind me telling you thith, Mithreth Abigail."

Moira turned and gestured to George to turn on the switch. George did so, and the dungeon was suddenly filled with the sound of "The Teddy Bears' Picnic."

"All right, pass the rattle around," Moira ordered the men. She walked across the dungeon and inspected the various implements for whacking men's bottoms. She chose a fine old English cane and walked back to the pit, just as George turned the music off again without warning.

Tommy had just been passing the rattle to Sammy. Both of them let out a squeal of dismay and dropped the rattle into the plastic straw.

"All right," said Moira, brandishing the cane sternly, "which one of you was holding that rattle when the music stopped?"

"He was!" shouted Tommy, pointing to Sammy. "I gave it to him!"

"No you didn't!" Sammy squealed. "You still had it in your hand!"

"You liar!" screamed Tommy. "You rotten sneaky little liar!"

"All right, that's enough! Both of you come up here." Moira pointed to the floor at her feet.

Putting on a good show of reluctance, the two men shambled up out of the pit, pouting and making faces at each other. Moira grabbed Tommy by the ear and forced him down onto his knees in front of her. Then she took hold of Sammy by the back of his neck and forced him down onto the flagstones too.

She walked behind them. Both men were wearing shorts. "Bend forward and lift those fat asses," Moira snapped. They quickly obeyed her. She grabbed their shorts and jerked them down, revealing the plump white flesh of their buttocks. "This is what happens to naughty boys like you," she said with relish. And she whipped first one of them with the cane, then the other.

All the others, including George, watched in wide-eyed silence as Moira raised the cane high, then swung it whistling through the air. Again and again it smacked into the men's lily-white skin, making the flesh jump. Both overgrown babies were soon bawling authentic tears. And at the same time, both of them were soon developing authentic hard-ons. Tommy, in fact, got so excited he had a spontaneous orgasm, jism spurting out of his cock and making a little gooey white puddle on the stone floor. Sammy, meanwhile, started furtively masturbating.

"Stop that!" Moira shouted at him. "Yes, you! Stop that at once! Stand up!"

Sammy stood up and hung his head.

"Hold out your hand!"

He held it out guiltily.

"Is that the hand you were using to touch your cock?"

"Yes, ma'am." He was wearing a mask, so his voice was muffled and barely audible.

Moira wielded the cane and hit Sammy sharply across the palm of his hand. He squealed in distress. She grabbed his wrist to stop him from pulling his hand away, and hit him five more times. With each blow, he squealed louder and his knees shook. The last blow somehow had the effect of bringing him to orgasm; semen spurted and dribbled from his cock, and made another puddle on the floor.

"You children disgust me!" Moira shouted. "Both of you, clean up those messes you made. Immediately!"

They got back down on their knees. Tommy started using the hem of his Junior Jogger T-shirt.

"Not with that!" Moira shouted. "You'll use your tongues. Go on, lick up that semen!"

"But the floor's dirty," Sammy whined.

"It won't be when you've finished," Moira snapped, and caned his bottom twice more. "That's for answering back."

She stood and waited while the two men lapped up their own juices. Then she nudged their fat flesh with the toe of her boot and pushed them back into the pit.

"George!" she called over her shoulder. "Start the music again." She surveyed her prisoners. Tommy and Sammy were both red in the face, their eyes bright with guilty pleasure. "Let's see who else needs to be given a caning," said Moira, with obvious satisfaction.

The rattle was passed from hand to hand once more. Moira repeated her punishment scene when the music stopped; this time Billy was the victim. She punished each of the men in turn, until finally, Herman Berman was the only one who hadn't been given the treatment.

"All right, now," said Moira. "I know that Hermie has been particularly bad. I saw him myself, downstairs, drinking liquor. Isn't that right, Hermie?" She walked around the edge of the pit, reached down, and grabbed Berman by his ear.

"Ow!" he squealed. "Ow, ow, let go my ear!"

"I asked you a question, Hermie," Moira persisted.

"Ow, ow! Oh, yes! Please! It's true! I admit it!"

"Just as I thought," Moira said. "Now, since Hermie has been so very, very naughty, I want to keep him here and punish him in private. All the rest of you, you can leave."

The others glanced at each other, and at Herman, in confusion. Evidently this wasn't the way things usually went.

"Mistress Abigail is a guest mistress," Berman explained, dropping his baby-voice for a moment.

"I never normally offer this kind of service to strangers," Moira told them. "Just as a favor to Hermie, here."

One by one the men got up out of the pit. Moira waited by the door from the dungeon to the study. She saw where the men had left their everyday clothes hanging on pegs on the stone wall by the exit. "Pick up your clothes and say 'Thank you for punishing me, mistress,'" she ordered them.

Obediently they filed past her and thanked her, blushing in embarrassment. Danny, the last of the men, lingered after the rest. "That was one of the most satisfying humiliations I've ever had," he told Moira in a furtive, eager voice. "I'd pay you five hundred a session, if you'd be willing—"

"Out of the question," she interrupted him. "This was purely as a favor to Mr. Berman."

"I'd go as high as a thousand," he persisted. "Just if you'd paddle my ass and tell me what a smelly little creep I am, once a week—"

"No!" Moira snapped, and gestured to the door.

He sighed in disappointment, and left.

"All right," said Moira, walking back to where Berman was in the pit. "Get up, you! And take off those diapers. Are they dirty?"

"Yes, mithreth," he lisped.

"Disgusting!" Moira exclaimed. "Go over there to the trestle." She selected some leather restraints from a rack on the wall and buckled one around each of Berman's wrists and ankles. Then she made him bend over the trestle. She chained his ankles to metal rings set in the stone floor on one side of the trestle, and his wrists to rings set in the floor on the other side of it.

"That's good," she said, admiring the way his bending over the trestle resulted in his ass sticking up in the air. "For you, Hermie, since you've been so naughty, I have an especially degrading humiliation. I'm going to get my sex-slave George to beat you. Frankly, you disgust me so much, I couldn't bear to beat you myself."

"Oh no, mithreth!" Berman twisted and tugged at his shackles. "Oh no, no!"

"George, come here!" ordered Moira. She handed him a cat-o'-nine-tails. "Whip his backside with that."

George took it from her. "Really, Moira?"

"Of course, you dummy!" She walked around to the other side of the trestle and grabbed Berman's head in her hands. She tilted his face up to look at her. "Meanwhile, Hermie, you will suck my nipples." She pulled a nearby stool over and sat down on it. Then she unlaced the top of her leather costume and pulled her breasts up and out of it. "I saw you staring at my tits," she went on. "Don't try to deny it, you bad, bad boy! I expect you'd like to touch them in your dirty little hands, wouldn't you? Admit it!"

"Yes, oh yes, it's all true," he whimpered, so excited he forgot to lisp.

"Ten lashes, for even thinking such a dirty thought!" Moira snapped. "Go on, George, don't just stand there!"

"Oh. Yes, right away," he said, and wielded the cat-'o-nine-tails. Its leather thongs swung down and smacked across Berman's bottom.

"Harder than that! Put some muscle into it!"

"Yes, Moira." He moved to obey. This time the leather thongs hit harder, and Berman gave a little gasp.

"Little babies like you mustn't think sexy thoughts about a lady's breasts," Moira said as George continued beating Berman's ass. "Little babies like you, Hermie, are only allowed to kiss and suck a lady's breasts. Come on, now." And she pushed her left breast into Berman's face.

He grunted and gasped at the treatment George was giving him. But then, craning his neck, he closed his lips around Moira's nipple and started sucking on it eagerly.

George stopped wielding the cat. He saw what Moira was doing with Berman and his face clouded with resentment.

"George!" Moira called to him warningly. "Are you getting jealous again?"

He sulked and didn't answer.

"That does it!" Moira exclaimed. She stood up, jerking her nipple out of Berman's mouth. "George, take that stupid doggie costume off and bend over the trestle beside Hermie, here. Immediately!"

"Oh no, mistress!" He shrank back from her.

"You heard me, George!"

He gulped. He fumbled with the fastenings of his costume. Meanwhile, Moira went and found some more leather restraints. Within minutes she had George spread-eagled over the trestle in exactly the same position as Berman, beside him.

"Now!" Moira cried, hefting the cat-o'-nine-tails. "Now I can teach you both a lesson, simultaneously." And she

55

brought the cat down in a wide arc that spread its long leather thongs across both George's and Berman's bottoms.

The two men twitched and yelped. Moira kept up the punishment in a heavy rhythm, till her arm felt heavy and her muscles ached. Then she dropped the cat, went back and sat down on the stool in front of the men. She was breathing hard from the exertion. She grabbed George and Berman, each by the hair, and tilted their heads up. "One nipple each, now," she said with delight. "Come along, babies And don't stop till I tell you to stop!"

She guided one of her nipples into George's mouth, and one into Berman's. Together they sucked at the buds of flesh, tongued and licked and did all they could for her. Moira was already feeling horny from having the two men totally under her power. She reached down, unlaced the crotch of her costume, and slid her hand in. She started masturbating quickly.

"Suck harder!" she commanded the men. "Yes! Oh, yes! Come on, George, he's doing it better than you! Lap with your tongue! Move your lips more! Ah, yes! Yes! Yeees!"

She stiffened as her orgasm hit her. She pushed her breasts into the men's faces, smothering them. "Suck!" she screamed at them. "Suck! Suck!" She vented a great scream of passion. And then, as the orgasm subsided, she pulled back.

For a moment the only sound in the dungeon was of male and female heavy breathing. Then, languorously, Moira stood up. She laced her costume shut again, at the crotch and over her breasts. Taking her time, she wandered around behind the men, and undid their restraints. She noted with satisfaction that both George and Berman had bright red asses.

"Thank you both for serving me," she told them. "You may kiss my boots."

Berman eagerly got down on his knees and started slobbering over the black leather.

"You, too, George!" Moira snapped.

Reluctantly George followed suit. He seemed to resent having to share her with the other man.

Moira went and sat back down on the stool. She put her hands on her hips. Suddenly she laughed, dropping her stern act. "God, I'm worn out!" she said.

Chapter Seven

Realizing that the role-playing was over, Herman Berman got up, walked to one corner of the dungeon, and took a brown cashmere robe out of a concealed closet. He came back, belting the robe. He no longer looked the part of Hermie, the bad little boy. Suddenly he was his everyday self again: Herman the movie mogul.

"I got to tell you, Abigail," he said to Moira, "that was just great. Loved every minute. You know, I remember back when you made those ten-minute one-hand movies for me. . . . What was it, six, eight years ago? Back when you were still in acting school and I was doing peep-show loops. You were the sexiest—"

"Herman," Moira interrupted him, now that she had learned his and Abigail's guilty little secret. "Herman, since you seem slightly more sober than you did before, let me try to tell you again what I tried to tell you outside. I am not Abigail. I am Abigail's twin sister, Moira. My god, I run a successful management business. You ought to have heard of me "

"No kidding," said Berman, putting his hands on his hips. "Sure, I've heard of you. I mean, I knew Abby had a sister, and her sister was Moira, who managed Abby's career. But I didn't know you and Abby was twins. Izzat why you dye your hair black? So's people don't get the two of you mixed up?"

"Correct," Moira said, with a professional smile. She gestured to George, who was standing in the background, naked, with his hands over his crotch. "That's my assistant, George. You understand, Herman, we all have our little secrets, here."

"Uh-huh. Sure." He nodded.

"Do you have another robe, for George?" Moira went on. "So he doesn't have to put on that ridiculous dog costume again."

"Of course. In fact I got some proper clothes he can wear," said Berman. "Come on, let's go get 'em. The dungeon's no place to talk." He led the way out, into his study. He paused to turn off the neon candles in the dungeon and close its secret bookcase-door, then showed Moira and George through to his master bedroom.

It was a huge expanse of white shag carpet as deep as unmowed grass, with white satin wallpaper, white velvet drapes, a white, ivory dressing table, a king-size bed covered in white yak fur, and two chairs upholstered in white polar-bear hide. The only thing that wasn't white was the ceiling, which was completely paneled in mirrors.

Berman opened a walk-in closet and pulled out some clothes for George. George accepted the garments without a word; he seemed to be sulking again, at having had to share his mistress's attentions with the other man.

"As I understand it, Herman," said Moira, "you've completely quit the hard-core pornography business."

Berman threw some white satin pillows on the bed, then sprawled among them. He gestured for Moira and George to make themselves comfortable on the chairs. "Yeah, I quit it. Of course, you know, the old movies still bring in some bucks. *Nympho Nancy* and *Teenage Twats* have become classics, for instance. They're showing like forever, here in L.A., and in New York, and there's some cut versions in London, I understand. The distributors are all crooked, but I screw the royalties out of 'em every six months or so. Still, apart from that, it's true I'm steer-

ing clear of sex activities. Aside from my own private life."
He grinned.

"Well, we all have our recreational vices," Moira said
smoothly.

"Yeah. Indeed we do." He chuckled. "I'll tell ya, Moira,
I don't know a single guy in this business who doesn't
have some kind of kinky weirdness. What the hell, most
of them are harmless."

Moira gave Berman a stiff smile. She seemed to find
him a little low class for her tastes. "Indeed," she said
blandly.

Berman stared at her for a moment longer with half-
closed eyes. "You're really something," he murmured.
"Just as pretty as your sister, but with claws. I like that in
a woman, I don't mind telling you. How's your management business? Doing well, is it? I'll tell ya, Moira, if you
ever need any help from me . . . I mean, I could be very
generous to you, understand me? Very generous . . . to a
woman who knows how to do what you, ah, know how
to do to a man."

George, sitting in the other chair, drew in his breath
sharply.

Moira glanced at him. "George!" she snapped warningly. She turned back to Berman. "You must excuse
George. He gets terribly jealous. God knows, I've tried
to cure him of it. I've tried all kinds of, ah, corrective
measures." She glanced back at George and was pleased
to see his face turn red with embarrassment.

"I'll bet you have," Berman said, obviously getting off
on imagining what Moira might have done. "Anyway, ah,
Moira, just remember what I said . . . if you ever need
some favors from me. Okay?"

Moira paused. She regarded Berman thoughtfully for
a moment. "Didn't I read, in *Variety* last week, something about a production you're doing . . . you had trouble
with the woman playing the leading role?"

"Yeah," said Berman. "Had to fire her, day before

yesterday. Helen Hingley. Jesus Christ, what a little prima donna. Like dealing with Maria Callas, except she got no talent to speak of. We kicked her out, for contract violations."

"I suppose it's too soon for you to have hired a replacement," Moira continued smoothly.

Berman shrugged. "My people are working on it."

Moira stood up. She paced to and fro, planting her black boots daintily in the deep white carpet. "Herman, dear, I do believe we may be able to make a deal. George! Wait outside for me, in the car. And don't worry your little head about me, sweetie pie. I can assure you that nothing indiscreet will happen between Mr. Berman and myself while you're out of the room."

"That's too bad," Berman said with a grin.

George stood up. He glanced quickly at Moira, then left, grim-faced.

When he had gone out and closed the door, Moira went and sat on the edge of the bed. "You know, Herman," she said softly and sweetly, "I think my sister Abigail would be just perfect as a replacement for that awful Helen Hingley person. In— What was the title of your movie, again?"

"We're calling it *Some Sweet Summer*. Romantic picture. Very romantic."

"Yes, of course. Can't you see Abigail in the role? By coincidence, she's just finished work on her last picture, and we've been looking for a suitable property for her. Something mature, but tasteful."

"I hear Abigail's a bitch to work with," Berman said.

"Oh, no no no!" Moira laughed gaily. "I mean, she and I sometimes have our differences—you know how sisters are!—but professionally, she's an angel." She smiled and stared into Berman's eyes. Then, as if on impulse, she reached out and closed her hand over his. "If Abigail and myself became involved with Herman Berman Productions, I know it would be a very rewarding partnership.

Rewarding for her, and also for me—and for you, too . . . Hermie."

When Moira joined George, outside in her Rolls-Royce, she was in a very cheerful mood. "Thanks for waiting for me, George dear," she said, as if George had had any choice in the matter. She kissed him on the cheek. "You are so sweet to me."

"Why did you ask me to leave?" he complained.

"There are some things, sweetie pie, that simply have to be discussed in private. That's all. I didn't want Herman feeling inhibited by your sitting there looking so moody, and resenting his every word. Don't you see?"

"No," George answered.

Moira sighed and drummed her fingers in exasperation. "George, I do declare—"

"I've had enough," he mumbled sullenly. "I've decided, Moira. I'm quitting. I can't put up with any more of the way you humiliate me."

"Oh, Jesus Christ, not this scene again," she exclaimed. "I remember the last time, in New York. My god, I hope we don't have to go through a rerun of that whole production. All your dramatic pronouncements, and then you came crawling back two days later."

"I did not! You asked me to come back!"

"George, dear George." She took his face between her hands and glared at him. He wasn't particularly handsome, that was for sure, with lank, brown hair and a shade too much flesh on him, like a slightly overgrown, overly serious college student. He wasn't especially sexy, but he was such a useful secretary; and when he wasn't throwing his jealous fits, he was completely devoted to her. The ideal live-in sex-slave, she had to admit. Moira sighed. Then, impulsively, she kissed him on his pouting lips.

George stared at her disconcertedly. She hardly ever—almost never—did that.

"Perhaps I have been a little unkind to you tonight," she said, making her voice sound quiet and concerned. She reached down for the fly of the large baggy pants that Herman Berman had given him. She undid the zipper expertly, and slid her hand inside. "I mean, you never even got your little rocks off, did you, honey?" She found his cock and started fondling it.

"You can't get around me that easily," he told her. He tugged at her wrist. "Moira, I mean it. I've had enough. I — Ow!" he cried out as she reached up with her other hand, grabbed him by the hair, and pulled his head back.

"You just sit there and enjoy this," Moira told him. She kept hold of his hair with one hand and started masturbating him briskly with the other.

"No!" George protested, trying to get her to let go of his hair. "Stop it!"

With satisfaction, Moira pulled his cock out of the fly of his pants and found it was fully erect. She slid around and sat on George's lap, there in the front seat of the Rolls, facing him. His cock stood up firm and hard, just in front of her crotch.

Moira quickly unlaced her leather costume, starting at the top, pulling the leather slowly away from her plump breasts. They fell out almost in George's face. He had stopped struggling now; she knew she'd gotten him so horny all through the evening, he was undoubtedly desperate for sex with her.

She unlaced the rest of the front of the leather costume, down to her vagina. "Want to fuck me, George?" she cooed to him. "Want me to sit on your cock? Hmm? Don't you want to feel it pushing slowly into my tight little pussy? Or, how about if I start rubbing my tits against your chest? Would you like that?" She grabbed his hair again and tilted his head back and kissed him hard. She pushed her tongue into his mouth and fluttered it from side to side. She took one of his hands and guided it to her tits; helplessly he grasped the soft flesh. She felt his resistance melting away.

Moira got up on her knees. She found his cock and guided it inside her. She sat down on it, trapping the whole length of it in her cunt. She wriggled to and fro.

"No," George protested feebly. "No, I won't—"

"Oh yes you will," Moira told him. She unbuttoned the front of his shirt, then pressed her naked breasts against his chest. She rubbed her body across his, and shifted her hips up and down, up and down, fucking herself on him. Then she brought her hands up and raked her fingernails over George's nipples. "You want it, George dear. Just the way you always do."

He didn't say anything more. He simply sat there, with his eyes closed. He took deep breaths through his mouth. He groaned.

Moira bounced up and down on his cock, feeling it plunge deep inside her. She raked her fingernails down his chest again, harder this time. Somehow the mild pain turned him on; she felt his cock swell larger inside her. She felt his muscles tense and his hips thrust up under her.

"Tell me how much you want me," she commanded him. She clenched her fingers and dug her long nails in around each of his nipples. "Tell me!"

"I want you," he gasped.

"You want me a lot, don't you, George?" She dug her nails in harder.

This time he did not reply. Moira slowed the movement of her hips, then lifted them as if she were going to pull herself off him. George gasped and tried to raise himself to keep his cock inside her.

Moira tantalized him, holding herself so that only the very tip of his cock was allowed within her. "You want me a lot, don't you, George," she repeated.

"I . . . want you a lot," he gasped, and he clutched himself against her, shamelessly.

Moira smiled in quiet triumph. She resumed her up-and-down motion on him. She increased the speed, and watched him grimace with desire for her. She dug her nails into his skin again and felt him flinch in her grip. "Come!" she told him. "Come, George!"

And he came. His hips jerked, and he turned his head from side to side, groaning. His cock spasmed inside her. He clenched his fists, then went limp as the orgasm subsided.

Moira pulled herself quickly off him. She opened the glove compartment, took out some Kleenex, and mopped herself, then him. She laced up her leather outfit while George sat slumped in his seat, his eyes closed, his arms lying limply by his sides, his cock lying limply in the fly of his pants.

Moira turned on the interior light of the Rolls and checked her appearance in the driving miror. Then she sat down in the passenger seat, reached across, and tucked George's penis neatly back in his pants. "Come along now, George," she told him. "It's time to go home."

Slowly George opened his eyes. He stared at Moira woefully for a moment.

"What's the matter, didn't you enjoy it?" Moira asked him.

He nodded reluctantly. Then, still looking glum, he started the car's engine and turned on the headlights. He stared ahead through the windshield, but didn't put the Rolls in gear. He swallowed hard, then cleared his throat. "Did you have sex with Berman up there?" he asked dully.

"No," said Moira. "I did not."

"You're going to, though," said George. "That's the deal, isn't it? He gives Abigail the movie role, and in return you—"

"Drive us home, George," Moira interrupted sharply. "I've let you fuck me, I've done all I can for you and your pathetic bruised little ego. Now, if you don't behave yourself, I really will lose my temper with you." She peered through the windshield at the wide expanse of Berman's private parking lot. "Let's get moving, shall we? And for god's sake, be careful. Those stupid butlers have left unconscious guests lying all over the gravel."

Chapter Eight

Cruising down the freeway in her Mercedes the next afternoon, Abigail switched restlessly from lane to lane and tuned the radio from station to station as if nothing was quite the way she wanted it. She hadn't been able to decide what to wear, she'd snapped at Brad when he telephoned earlier, and now she didn't even know why she was bothering to meet Lord Whatever-his-name-was at the Beverly Wilshire. It seemed so stupid; she already had Brad, and he was absolutely devoted to her. What did she need in some stuck-up British snob? And an afternoon rendezvous at a hotel was so damned tacky.

She left her car for the valet to park and walked into the Polo Lounge. The place was always stuffed with tourists and movie producers; she despised both social groups equally. The lounge was noisy and smelled of booze and cigars.

Abigail tapped her foot. She couldn't see Barrington. If he was standing her up—

She felt a hand on her shoulder and turned quickly. It was him, wearing a heavy Scottish tweed suit, very British and respectable but hopelessly impractical in the Los Angeles climate.

"I don't know why you picked this place," Abigail complained without any preliminaries. "There are no available tables, and—"

"I should not be seen socializing with you," he interrupted her. "And I'm not entirely sure why I picked this place, myself. Will you come with me?" He took her arm and guided her into the hotel lobby.

Out by the elevators, she pulled her arm free from his grip. "Look," she said, "I don't really—"

"We can't talk here," he interrupted her.

She looked up at him. Despite herself, she remembered the way she'd felt with him the previous night. He had such a commanding presence; she didn't know whether it was his dignity, his cultural background, his good looks, or maybe just her imagination. But it made it hard for her to think straight. "So where do you want to talk?" she complained, still sounding testy but no longer quite so sure of herself.

"Upstairs." He took her arm again and quickly stepped with her into an elevator.

"But I don't really—" Abigail began again.

There were no other passengers in the elevator as its door closed and it started upward. Lord James Barrington took Abigail's face between his hands and kissed her hard on the mouth. "Just to refresh our memories," he said quietly.

Then the doors opened and he led Abigail out and down a corridor. She was no longer complaining; she looked confused.

Lord Barrington ushered her into his suite. It was lavishly large, cluttered with imitation antiques, dominated by a huge bed. "You were saying," he said as he closed the door, "that you didn't really . . . what?"

"I just think perhaps you were right last night," Abigail said in a subdued voice, avoiding his eyes, "when you said it could be one of those encounters we shouldn't try to repeat."

"Ah, I see." Lord Barrington went and turned up the air conditioner, then walked to the bed, removed his shoes, and lay back against the padded headboard. He watched Abigail as she briefly stared out the window, then paced back across the room.

"I have a perfectly good relationship with a guy who's totally hung up on me," she said. She stopped at the lavishly stocked bar and poured herself a Pernod and orange juice. "He gives me everything I want." She walked to the foot of the bed and stood sipping the drink and staring defiantly at Lord Barrington.

"And yet," he replied, "you did seem, shall I say, responsive to my overtures . . . last night."

"I went along with your so-called overtures because I was horny as hell, because of . . . because of a little scene that had been interrupted earlier. That's why." She paused, then added: "And I guess I kind of liked you."

Lord Barrington sighed. "Well, what am I supposed to conclude? That you came here today to tell me you didn't want to see me? In that case why didn't you simply phone and leave a message, instead?"

Abigail drained her glass and dumped it on a marble-topped, bow-fronted dressing table whose cheap veneer was embellished tastelessly with too much gold paint. "Oh, shit, I don't know."

"Do you want to leave?"

His voice was neutral, so far as she could tell. That damned British reserve of his. She shrugged. "Not especially."

"Then, perhaps you should come and sit here beside me," he said.

She looked at him and their eyes met. He stared at her steadily. Though he hadn't raised his voice or altered its tone, there was once again something commanding about it, as if he were so accustomed to having people do as he said the possibility of her defying him didn't even enter his head.

Slowly, taking her time about it, Abigail sauntered across the room. She flopped down beside him on the bed. "Well?" she asked.

In reply Lord Barrington took hold of her shoulders, pulled her against him, and kissed her hard. She felt the strength in his hands and in his body, and she smelled his cologne, and suddenly she found herself reliving their encounter together on the grass at Berman's party the previous night.

He held her as if she were a precious treasure: gently, so as not to mar her beauty, but firmly, to eliminate the chance of her taking herself away from him. He kissed her and kissed her, insistently pressing his lips to hers. He reached down and slid his hand under her skirt. Within moments his fingers had found their way inside her panties. He started expertly manipulating her clitoris.

Abigail broke the kiss for a moment and tugged at his wrist. "I really don't—" she began.

James Barrington caught her under her arms, lifted her, turned her, and pushed her down into the soft bed. He quickly unbuttoned the blouse she was wearing and pushed her bra up off her breasts. He started licking and sucking first one nipple, then the other. All the while, he continued to rub her clitoris with his finger.

Abigail swallowed hard. She realized there was no point in trying to maintain the pretense of not wanting him. Something about him was irresistible. She felt her breathing and her pulse speeding up. A warm flush crept into her cheeks. Her nipples and clitoris tingled from his attentions. Instinctively she found herself hugging him to her.

He stopped sucking her nipples, slid one hand behind her head, and kissed her again, drawing her lips up to his. His fingers clenched gently in her hair, so that she couldn't possibly pull away. His tongue pushed slowly into her mouth. He shifted the weight of his body onto hers until it was holding her down on the bed. She felt the long, hard shape of his cock pressing through his clothes.

He ceased touching her clitoris and moved that hand to her left breast. He pinched the nipple between his finger and thumb. "I want you, Abigail," he told her quietly. He pinched her nipple harder, till she drew in her breath sharply. "I want you," he repeated. He released his hold on her nipple for a moment. "When I truly desire something, Abigail, I never, never let it ... escape me."

And suddenly he pinched her nipple again, much harder than before. Abigail cried out in surprise at the stab of pain. But it was very brief, and somehow it only aroused her even more. The way he stared at her, his total concentration on her, his absolute determination to possess her—it all turned her on. She lay passively on her back, breathing hard, staring up at him. She'd lost all her self-control somehow, but she no longer cared.

He found the zipper of her skirt, loosened it, and pulled her skirt off. Then her underwear. "I'm sorry if I ... was moody, just now," she told him. "I guess I didn't like the way you got under my skin last night. I don't like any man to think he can manipulate me, or my feelings."

"I understand entirely," he told her. He stroked his finger down her cheek, then very lightly across her lips. "You are a spirited, independent woman," he went on. He started stripping off his clothes. "And I would never want you to be any other way. Except, of course, in the bedroom. Here, you play a subtler role. Here, for just a little while, you can enjoy sacrificing your resistance and your independence."

He stood naked in front of her. His body was firm and trim, his shoulders muscular. She guessed he exercised a lot, maybe riding horses on his country estate, or whatever it was he owned in England. Without any obvious embarrassment he fondled the length of his erect cock while he watched her stretched out on the bed before him. Then he kneeled on the bed between her legs.

"I hope you understand me, about the roles one takes, inside and outside of the bedroom," he said.

Abigail felt dazed. Her body was glowing with arousal, and it was hard for her to concentrate. "I hadn't thought about it that much," she said vaguely.

He edged forward, reached down, and pulled her hips

up toward him. "When you are outside," he told her, "you are your own woman." He rubbed the head of his cock between her labia. "But when you are here, in my bed—" He lunged into her suddenly, making Abigail cry out and grab hold of his shoulders. "Here, you are mine."

Chapter Nine

Lord Barrington fucked Abigail with a furious intensity. His aristocratic cock plunged in and out relentlessly. He wrapped one arm around her shoulders, the other around her hips, so that she could barely move and was helpless in his grip. He gave her what could only be described as a royal screwing.

Abigail closed her eyes and surrendered herself to the experience. She was very conscious of his powerful body, his strong hands, his hard and heavy breathing, and his hard and heavy cock thrusting into her. She clung to him, feeling fragile against his strength. His body smacked against hers, and the bed shook and shuddered beneath them both. She felt the sensations growing and growing, more and more intense. She moaned as she felt her orgasm coming close.

He paused then, in his frenetic lovemaking. He let go of her and raised himself over her with his arms out straight. He moved his hips gently from side to side, grinding slowly against her so that she continued to be aroused but didn't get any nearer to orgasm. His chest heaved as he got his breath back from the last few minutes of all-out fucking. His skin was filmed with sweat.

"Don't stop now," Abigail said in a small voice, opening her eyes and staring up at him.

"Stop? Why, certainly not," he said. He reached down

between his body and hers, and moistened his fingertip in the juices between her labia, where the fat shaft of his cock still moved just a little to and fro. Then he caressed her clitoris lightly. "Does that please you, my dear?"

She smiled uncertainly. "You know it does." She swallowed hard and felt all her muscles clench involuntarily as a sudden spasm of sensation rippled through her. She pushed her hips up to engulf the whole length of his cock, but he held himself away a little, tantalizing her just as he had tantalized her the previous night.

For a minute or two the only sound in the hotel room was his and her heavy breathing as he tickled her clitoris with his wet fingertip, rolling it up and down and from side to side while he watched the emotions in her face. Then he closed his other hand upon one of her plump breasts and squeezed the soft flesh. He rolled the nipple between finger and thumb while he continued toying with her clitoris, with his cock still buried inside her.

He felt her vagina clench on him. She arched her back, shivered, and gasped. He knew she was right on the edge of orgasm. He stopped touching her, took both hands away from her body, and lowered himself onto her. He jerked his hips and thrust his cock all the way in.

Abigail whimpered and tried to move under him, but his weight pinned her.

"Kiss me," he told her quietly.

She turned her head and pressed her lips against his. He held his mouth hard against hers. Their tongues met.

He jerked his lips, sending a sudden surge of erotic feelings pulsing through her from her clitoris. Again he jerked his hips, and again. And all the time he kept his mouth on hers.

Abigail felt herself trembling with sexual tension. She was so close to her climax, so very close. Each time he jerked his hips, jamming his groin against hers, he took her another little step nearer to coming. And the way he kept kissing her, his mouth clamped upon hers, took her

74

higher still. He kissed her so deeply, so totally, the kiss seemed to absorb her whole self.

Once more he pushed his crotch against hers. And this time it was the last stimulus she needed. Abigail felt all the tension suddenly let go inside her. She shivered uncontrollably. She clung to him, and tore her mouth free and screamed. She took great gasping breaths and shook to the pure pleasure that pulsed through her. It seemed to last forever.

When the last of her orgasm was over, he gently pulled out of her and turned her over facedown on the bed. She was past resisting. She was lost in a dizzy world of pure sensation.

He grabbed a pillow and inserted it under her belly so that her hips and ass were raised up into the air. He moved between her legs, nudged her knees further apart, grasped his cock, and put the head of it between her thighs.

Abigail let out a slow sigh as Lord Barrington guided his cock into her cunt. She had felt empty without it.

He started fucking her from behind in a slow but steady rhythm. He was kneeling between her legs and bending forward so that his chest brushed against her back. He reached under her and grabbed hold of her breasts. He held them firmly as he continued fucking her.

"You are so beautiful, Abigail," he said, pushing his cock into her. "Blond and beautiful." His cock slid in deep. "A Hollywood goddess." He fucked her relentlessly. "Soft and warm and sexy . . ." His fingers clenched on her tits. "And mine." He fucked her harder. "At this moment you are mine. Are you not?" His fingers dug into her breasts. "Aren't you mine, Abigail?"

She winced, but didn't tell him to stop. She nodded wordlessly, her cheek pressed into the sheets of the bed.

"Mine. You give your beauty all to me," Lord Barrington said in a rising voice. His hips moved in a series of little jerks. He grunted and gasped. His fingers clenched even harder on her breasts. "Mine!" he gasped again.

And then he came. She felt every little twitch of his

cock as he held it embedded in her. She heard him let out a long, impassioned groan of fulfillment.

And then, at last, he slumped down onto her, breathing hard.

There was a long pause. Then Lord Barrington rolled onto his back and lay beside Abigail. She squirmed onto her side and looked at his face. His eyes were closed and his features were composed. She traced her finger along his aristocratic profile: the high forehead, the long, straight nose, the firm mouth.

Then she sat up. She ran her fingers through her hair, trying to rake out some of the tangles. "That was something," she said in a distant, dreamy voice. "That was quite something, your lordship."

He reached out and drew her to him. She fell on top of him with her breasts squashed against his chest. "It didn't bother you that it was not particularly . . . casual?" he asked with an ironic smile.

Abigail looked away. "Guess not," she said. "Oh, hell, I don't feel like being flippant. You've gotten through to me, James." She kissed him quickly on the cheek. "And I'm not going to keep trying to deny it."

Then, as if embarrassed by what she'd just said, she got up and went quickly into the bathroom.

She came back a couple of minutes later with a bright, lively look in her eyes. "How would it be . . ." she said, then walked over and sat on the edge of the bed. She poked him playfully with her finger. "How would it be . . . if I came over and visited you some time, in jolly old England? Would you like that?" She ran her hand lightly across his chest.

He watched her for a moment. "It would be delightful, Abigail," he said slowly. "But awkward. The, ah, countess certainly would not approve."

Abigail frowned. "The what? I mean, the who?"

"The countess." Lord Barrington sat up and smoothed his thick, dark hair back from his forehead. "My wife, the Countess of Dorset. You do realize, Abigail, that I'm a married man."

There was an uncomfortable pause. Abigail forced a laugh. "No. No, I don't realize. Or I didn't, anyhow. I guess that's because you didn't tell me till now." She drew back from him abruptly and turned her head away from him.

"We've hardly known each other for very long," Lord Barrington said, choosing his words carefully. "Surely you don't blame me, Abigail, for failing to mention my wife until now."

Abigail sighed. Then she shrugged. "What the hell. No, I don't blame you. Well, it was nice while it lasted. I guess I won't get to have afternoon tea at Buckingham Palace, that's all." She forced a smile, stood up, and started putting on her clothes.

"We might possibly arrange a secret assignation," Lord Barrington told her.

Abigail shook her head. "I don't get off on sneaking around behind another woman's back."

"My wife is well aware that I, ah, have occasional encounters with other women," Lord Barrington persisted. "You see, she has no interest in the, ah, physical aspects of love. She understands that I have certain needs I must indulge elsewhere."

"Yeah, such as here." Abigail pulled the last of her clothes on. She looked in the mirror and combed her hair. "Look, no offense, but I really think I better get back home now. You were right, right all along; this was just one of those brief things . . ."

Lord Barrington quickly got off the bed and strode over to her. Still naked, he hugged her from behind. He kissed her neck. "I'm sorry, Abigail."

She turned in his arms. "Me too," she said in a small voice.

He kissed her on the mouth. It was very poignant, and she felt herself weakening. . . .

But no, that was no way to go. She had to get out of there, and fast.

She broke free from his embrace. "I gotta go," she said. "Sorry to run out on you like this, but— bye." And then, before he could say anything to change her mind, she opened the door and stepped out into the hallway. He couldn't come after her . . . he was naked. She ran down the hall and took the fire stairs rather than wait for an elevator. She knew she had to leave quickly; else she might never want to leave at all.

By the time she was parking her car back at her home, Abigail had thrust aside all the romantic yearnings Lord James Barrington had sparked in her. It wasn't going to be possible to have anything serious with him, so she had to forget about it, and that was that.

She locked her car and walked into her house. As she shut the front door behind her, the phone started ringing.

Maybe it's Brad calling, she thought to herself. That would be good: an evening with him, to clear away the last lingering memories of James Barrington.

She picked up the phone. "Hello?"

But it wasn't Brad. It was Moira.

"Abigail, dear," Moira cooed, in a voice that was meant to sound intimate but set Abigail's teeth on edge. "I've got great news for you!"

Abigail didn't answer right away. She picked up the phone and carried it to the living room couch. She sat down carefully. "What is it?" she asked, keeping her voice neutral.

"I have been having just the most wonderful day, dear, with your old pal Herman Berman," Moira said. "You know, I met him at his party last night. And guess what! He's offering you the female lead in *Some Sweet Summer*. I don't know if you read about it, but they had to fire Helen Hingley from the part when—"

"Yeah, I read about it," Abigail interrupted.

"Well, aren't you just thrilled? I mean, it's the ideal

movie! It's a romance, but it has an adult theme, just the kind of thing you've been wanting and—"

"They're shooting it in England, aren't they?" Abigail asked. She felt suddenly dizzy, as if the world were doing things to her that were completely out of her control.

"Why, yes!" Moira exclaimed. "You'll be over there for three whole months! Isn't that wonderful?"

"No," said Abigail. She pressed her fingers to her forehead.

"Whatever do you mean?" said Moira. The tone of her voice changed immediately. It developed a nasty, warning edge. "Good god, Abigail, are you going to tell me this isn't what you want?"

Abigail slumped back on the couch. She shook her head. She realized she was being stupid. It was stupid to mix up her personal and her business lives. "I'm sorry," she said mechanically. "You're absolutely right, it's a great part for me. I'd be crazy to turn it down."

"Well now, that's more what I expected you to say! But I haven't told you the best bit. I even got Hermie—I mean, Mr. Berman—to offer your boyfriend Brad one of the minor male roles. So he can be over there with you, for the whole time! Isn't that just great? You see how hard I work for you, Abby, dear?"

"Yes," said Abigail, blankly. She had a sudden, tormented vision of James Barrington's body close to hers; his cock inside her; his mouth— No, she had vowed to forget him. She shut her eyes and willed him out of her head.

But how could she forget him if she was going to his country, where the men all talked like him?

"Thanks, Moira," she said dully. "Thanks for everything. I guess this is all I could ever have asked for." And she put down the phone.

Chapter Ten

"How does this sound?" asked Brad. He got up out of his airplane seat and stood in the aisle of the first-class cabin of the 747. He held his script at arm's length and turned to face Abigail. "Good morning, Miss Simmons," he declaimed in a deep, booming voice. "Nice day." He paused for effect, then returned to his seat beside her. "Do you think that sounds right?" he asked her, back in his normal voice. "Or should I maybe make the accent sound less, ah, educated?"

"Jesus Christ," Abigail said. Her voice was slurred from the booze she'd been drinking. She closed her eyes.

"I just want to know what you think, Abigail. I mean, you don't have to make a big deal out of it."

"Me make a big deal out of it! My god, Brad, you've been fucking around with that same stupid line for a whole goddamn hour! You're driving me crazy! Shit, you're going to be playing an apartment-building doorman, not Hamlet!"

"All right, all right," he scowled, closed the script, and stared moodily at its cover.

"I need another drink," Abigail said. She leaned around and signaled to the stewardess.

"Another?" said Brad.

"Yeah," said Abigail.

Brad shifted uneasily. "Abby, you've been more or less

drunk for the whole of the past two days, ever since Berman's party. And you keep snapping at me, like I can't do a single thing right. What is it with you? What's wrong?"

"I'll tell you what's wrong. You keep asking me what's wrong. That's what's wrong."

"May I help you, Miss van Pelt?" said the stewardess, stopping beside Abigail's seat. "More champagne?"

"Now, here's someone who understands my needs!" said Abigail. She held out her plastic wineglass and her arm weaved unsteadily from side to side.

"You know, I feel kind of silly saying this," said the stewardess, pouring the champagne. "But I have to tell you, Miss van Pelt, I've seen all your movies. Twice, some of them. I think you're really wonderful."

"How about that," said Abigail, taking a big swig from her glass. "That's nice. Nice of you to say that."

"Is there anything else I can get you?"

"Yeah. I'd like a couple lines of cocaine." Abigail laughed and then stopped herself, realizing she was losing control. She tried to regain a hold on herself. It was difficult; if she brought herself too far down to reality, she started remembering James Barrington.

"I'm sorry," she told the stewardess, noticing the young woman's disconcerted expression. "Didn't mean to shock you or anything. I was just joking, about the cocaine. You know?"

"Oh, that's okay," the stewardess said with a shy smile, "Actually," she leaned closer to Abigail, "a lot of us who work for the airline do coke when we work. It helps with the jet lag. I was just surprised that you— I mean, you acted all those innocent-little-girl roles in your movies, so I thought—"

"That's in the past," Abigail said. "And it was never the real me anyhow." She gestured to an empty seat just the other side of the aisle. "Can you sit down a minute?"

"Why, sure. I mean, thank you."

"Hey, Abigail." Brad tapped her shoulder. "I don't think this is smart," he murmured into her ear. "You're drunk and you don't know what you're saying, and careerwise—"

He stopped abruptly and grunted in pain as Abigail dug her elbow violently into his ribs. She turned back to the stewardess. "Don't worry about my boyfriend," she said. "He's a jerk. What's your name?"

"Sharon," the stewardess answered.

"Yeah? Tell me, Sharon," Abigail leaned closer, "is it true what they say? About what goes on with the stewardesses and the crew and everything? The mile-high club?"

Sharon paused, then smiled a secretive smile. She had a cute turned-up nose, short black hair, and blue eyes. She looked very young—maybe about twenty—but she gave Abigail a knowing look. "Maybe," she said carefully. "I guess if you want to know something, you'd have to be a bit more specific."

"All right. Did you ever make it with the pilot? In the cockpit, while the plane's flying?"

"Sure." Sharon's cheeks dimpled demurely.

"Yeah?" said Abigail. "How about during takeoff?"

Sharon hesitated. She lowered her voice. "Once. I gave him a blow job, out of Cincinnati."

"Really?" Abigail narrowed her eyes. "What about the other stewardesses? You ever make it with them?"

"Well, sometimes." Sharon ran just the tip of her tongue across her lower lip. "And sometimes with the passengers, too."

"Hmm." Abigail glanced around the first-class section she was sitting in. Most of the seats were empty. There were a couple of businessmen, an elderly lady; and Moira and George and Herman Berman were sitting two rows back. "I guess there's no one you'd be interested in on this trip."

Sharon paused to choose her words carefully. "Actually, there is one person," she said, staring directly into Abigail's eyes.

"No kidding." Abigail leaned closer, till her face was less than a foot away from Sharon's. "You sure are pretty," she said, her voice barely audible above the steady hiss of jet noise.

Sharon glanced down at the champagne bottle she was still holding. Then she looked directly back at Abigail. "They'll be turning the cabin lights out in a little while," she said. "I'll be back then. Why don't you keep this in the meantime?" She handed Abigail the half-full champagne bottle. Then she stood up. She smoothed her uniform and arched her back, emphasizing the shape of her breasts. Then, quickly, she walked back to the galley.

Abigail laughed and poured herself another drink.

"What was all that about?" Brad asked. "I couldn't hear what you were saying."

"Girl talk," said Abigail, and giggled. She drained her glass and filled it again.

Brad scowled. "I just don't understand you. You're really abusing your body, drinking like this. You're going to need all the strength you can get. This is a tough assignment, learning a whole role in just a matter of days."

"Oh, for fuck's sake," Abigail muttered. She stood up and walked down the aisle. "Herman!" she called, waving the bottle. "Want a refill?"

"We got our own entertainment here, Abby, honey," he said. He gestured to where he was spreading several six-inch lines of coke across the back of an airline safety-instructions leaflet. "Want in?"

Abigail slumped into a seat beside him. "Why, sure," she said. "That's just what I need."

"Got to pass the time somehow, right?" said Berman, snorting the first line.

"Yeah, this flight's a killer," Abigail said vaguely. "I hate doing it nonstop, LA to London. Ten fucking hours. Too bad your movie's so far behind schedule. Still," she went on, "we got some real open-minded flight attendants on this trip."

Berman snorted his second line and made throaty noises. He clenched his fists. His chest heaved and his face turned red. He let out a deep breath and grinned. "You been lining up a cute little stewardess for me?"

Abigail shook her head. "Not for you. For me," she said, taking the coke and his solid silver Tiffany snorting tube.

Berman threw his head back and roared with laughter. "You ain't changed a bit, Abby," he said. "Not since . . . since those times we don't talk about, right?" He turned to Moira. "Right?"

"I wouldn't know about that, Herman, dear," she said with a thin smile. She patted his cheek condescendingly.

Berman studied her with half-closed eyes. He was drunk, and he was high on the coke. "You look . . . good enough to eat," he said slowly. His hand reached for Moira's crotch.

"Behave yourself!" Moira snapped. She slapped him hard across his wrist. Then she reached in her purse and pulled out a little book. "That's another black mark, Hermie," she told him, making a note in the book. "I simply can't believe how badly you've been behaving today. I'm going to have to be very strict with you, when we get to London."

Herman turned and winked at Abigail. "Your sister, here, is a real ball-breaker," he murmured. He swallowed hard, obviously feeling aroused. He leaned closer to Abigail. "Which is just the way I like 'em!" he confided, and started chuckling dementedly.

"I guess you haven't changed, either," Abigail said, remembering some of the sleazier scenes she'd seen Berman in, back in her days making porno loops for him.

"Have you finished, dear?" Moira called across to Abigail.

"What?"

"With the candy, my dear," said Moira, with an impatient edge to her voice. Then, seeing that Abigail still didn't understand: "The nose candy."

"Oh," Abigail turned her attention to the coke, inhaled her share, then handed the remainder to her sister. She noticed George sitting in the far seat with an expression of resentment and disdain. "Hey, George, don't you want some too?"

"It's bad for his sinuses," Moira cut in quickly before George had time to answer. She seized the coke and snorted all the rest of it greedily.

Abigail walked clumsily around to the second aisle. She sat on the armrest of George's seat. "Hey, what's up?" she asked him. "How about a little drink?" She offered the bottle of champagne.

"Thanks," said George, accepting the bottle from her. He upended it to his mouth and kept swallowing till it was completely empty.

Abigail frowned at him. "Drowning your sorrows, huh?"

"You could put it like that." He scowled.

"You shouldn't get so uptight about Moira playing around," said Abigail. "She always comes back to you, you know."

George shrugged. "We all have things that get to us. Don't we?" He gave Abigail a hard look.

"You're not kidding," Abigail said. "I'll tell you about it sometime." And she half thought she might. George was about the only person she could imagine confiding in about how she'd gotten so hung up on James Barrington.

"Abby, honey!" Berman interrupted from across the cabin. "Want another?" He was busily laying out more fine white powder.

"Shit, why not," said Abigail. "I mean, if you're going to get fucked up," she said, ignoring a shocked look from one of the businessmen in a nearby seat, "you may as well get totally fucked up, right?" She started back to Berman.

At that moment the cabin lights dimmed. "This concludes the evening entertainment portion of our flight," said a voice over the intercom. "Please make yourselves comfortable. We'll be leaving the main lights off for the next five hours, to enable those of you who wish to sleep to do so. Thank you."

"And to enable those of us who wish to party, to have our fun in privacy," said a soft voice from behind Abigail.

Abigail turned. She saw a slim, petite figure in the semi-dark cabin. "Sharon?"

"Who else?" The young stewardess reached out and stroked her fingers very lightly across Abigail's cheek.

Abigail caught Sharon's wrist and kissed her fingers. "Come join us," she said, and led her to Berman. He'd turned on his reading light in order to finish cutting the new portion of coke.

"Sharon, this is Mr. Berman. He's the producer of the movie I'm going to be making in England."

"Hi, honey," said Berman. "Hey, do you ever get headaches in your line of work? On account of the high altitude and all?"

Sharon blinked. "Sometimes, I guess."

"Yeah." Berman nodded wisely. "Just as I thought. You better try some of this." He handed Sharon the cocaine. "It's a special homeopathic remedy. I get it from my doctor in Florida." He chuckled and his chest heaved.

"Oh, Hermie!" said Moira, and started laughing with him, as though this were the funniest joke she'd ever heard.

Sharon snorted her share and reluctantly handed the rest back to Berman. He took it from her, but in the dim light he fumbled it. The precious powder spilled all over the floor.

"Oh, my god!" Moira screamed. "This is terrible!"

"What's happening?" One of the other passengers from a few rows back had suddenly awakened. "What's wrong? Something wrong with the plane?"

"No, go back to sleep, sir," Sharon said, returning to her stewardess role. She sniffed and dabbed at her nose. "Someone dropped something, that's all."

"Shhh," Berman was telling Moira.

"Shhh yourself," Moira told him, and started giggling again.

"I'd better deal with this," said Abigail. She fell down on her knees and started sniffing across the airplane carpet like a vacuum cleaner, scavenging the spilled coke.

"I'll help," Sharon said, and joined her.

Abigail felt the girl's young body close to hers, smelled her perfume, saw her face. Together, laughing, their cheeks almost touching, they inhaled whatever coke they could find. Then they both looked at each other, and suddenly Sharon reached for Abigail and kissed her hard on the mouth.

Abigail was dizzy. The plane seemed to be moving under her. She found herself slumping down on her back in the aisle, with Sharon leaning over her, kissing her insistently. The girl's tongue probed eagerly into Abigail's mouth. Her hands expertly unbuttoned Abigail's blouse and reached inside. She slid her fingers inside Abigail's bra and closed her fingers around her breasts.

"We better get off the floor," Abigail said, trying to keep some sense of what the hell was going on. She tried to stand up. Her blouse was undone, and her skirt was up around her hips. She slumped onto some nearby seats, which luckily turned out to be vacant.

Sharon reached up to open a locker and pulled out an airline blanket. She spread it expertly across Abigail, then lifted the edge and dived under it. There under the blanket, giggling, she hugged Abigail and managed to unhook her bra. Her fingers stroked Abigail's tits and caressed her nipples, lightly, gently, teasingly—so different from James Barrington's firm touch. But Abigail wasn't going to let herself think about that.

Sharon unbuttoned her uniform and pressed her own naked breasts against Abigail's. "I can't believe it," she whispered in Abigail's ear. "I can't believe I'm actually making it with you. After seeing all those movies of you. Just the thought of it makes me so wet inside. Feel!" She grabbed Abigail's hand and thrust it under her skirt.

Abigail discovered the girl had prudently removed her panties beforehand. Abigail's fingers encountered Sharon's naked crotch. She felt the folds of soft skin, the clitoris standing up swollen and hard. She slid her fingers inside Sharon's warm, wet pussy.

"Oh!" Sharon cried. Her hands grabbed at Abigail. "Oh Christ! Yes!" Her body writhing, alive with sexual energy.

Abigail masturbated Sharon quickly, moving her fingers inside her and rubbing her clitoris with her thumb. Sharon's breath came in little gasps. Abigail squirmed around on the soft first-class airplane seats. Her elbow hit the recline button and the back of the seat suddenly tilted under her. The two women slumped down, Abigail's fingers still working furiously in Sharon's crotch.

Sharon made whimpering noises. Abigail pressed her mouth to Sharon's, partly because she was afraid the girl's noises would attract attention.

Sharon's young body shivered and shook. She fervently returned Abigail's kiss. Then, without warning, she came.

Her body bucked and twisted, and she clutched at Abigail. Her fingers raked across Abigail's breasts. She grabbed Abigail's hand and forced it harder against her clitoris. She writhed and fell off the seats onto the floor. Abigail's fingers were still inside the girl, and even down there on the floor she kept coming and coming. At last, finally, her orgasm tapered off and she lay panting.

"Well!" said a voice. Moira's voice. "Well now, if you two have finished for a minute," Moira went on, standing over them, "Hermie and I have thought of the greatest party game we can all play together!"

Chapter Eleven

"We couldn't help noticing," said Moira, trying to keep her voice low pitched and confidential, "how very quickly you reached orgasm, Sharon."

Sharon had got up off the floor and was furtively buttoning her uniform. "My god, was it that obvious?" She glanced around anxiously. "I told the other flight attendants to leave first class to me for the next hour or so—and I think they got the message—but do you think any of the passengers noticed what was going on?"

"If any of 'em causes any trouble I'll bust 'em on the nose!" Herman Berman interrupted loudly. He tried to stand up, then fell back into his seat, chuckling to himself.

"The passengers all went to sleep," Moira told Sharon quietly. She gave Sharon a reassuring pat on her shoulder. "Except for George and Brad, who are up there together." She nodded toward the front.

"Party-poopers!" exclaimed Berman, with another guffaw.

Moira turned to him and poked him savagely in the ribs. "Hermie, if you don't shut the fuck up," she hissed at him, "I'll get my riding crop and beat the shit out of you!"

"Now?" said Berman, eagerly. "Now? Really?"

Moira rolled her eyes. She looked at Sharon and Abigail. Then, despite herself, she covered her mouth and giggled. The drink and drugs she'd consumed had made her almost human. "Anyway," she went on, "I told Hermie I could climax that fast myself. But it all depended on who went down on me. I said, in my experience most women do it better than men. After all, they know how, from the inside out, so to speak."

"Are you suggesting," Sharon interrupted quickly, "we have a race?"

"Exactly!" Moira clapped her hands in delight.

"Who eats who?" Sharon asked eagerly.

"Well, seeing that Abigail and myself are identical twins, I think it would be a very fair test if we are the ones who get eaten. That way, the first one of us who comes is obviously the one who's been treated best."

"Great!" said Sharon. "I'll do Abigail, and your Mr. Berman can do you."

"If he's still capable," said Moira, looking at Herman with a mixture of doubt and despair.

"Why don't you go get George?" said Abigail.

"No! No, I can out-lick any goddamn pansy-faced male secretary, by god," said Berman. "And anyhow, I've been wanting to suck your pussy for hours." He lunged toward Moira's crotch.

"Hey, no fair!" said Abigail. "Don't jump the gun!"

"He's so eager, isn't he, the dear boy," said Moira. She patted Berman's balding head, where he had slumped down on the floor in front of her and was pawing her thighs. "It's hard to refuse him, isn't it? Actually, I would let George have a turn, but he's gone into such a snit I really can't be bothered with him."

"All right," said Abigail. "Let's get organized here." She noted that Berman was already in position, sprawled on the floor, his head near Moira's crotch, his legs sticking out into the aisle. The seat next to Moira was empty, and the other aisle was beyond that. "Come on, Sharon," Abigail muttered. She grabbed the stewardess's hand and staggered around to the seat beside Moira. She slumped into it and spread her legs. Sharon kneeled down in front of her.

"Ready?" said Moira.

"Hell, no, I have to take my panties off," said Abigail. She slipped out of the underwear and threw it carelessly across the cabin. It landed in the lap of the elderly lady sleeping at the back. She slumbered on without noticing.

"To your marks!" whispered Moira. She guided Berman's head between her thighs, but kept her hand over her crotch to prevent him from licking her just yet.

Abigail slid her hands behind Sharon's neck and urged the girl's head forward. Sharon didn't need much urging.

"All right, get set!" Moira went on. "Now, go!"

It suddenly became very quiet. The only sound was the steady jet noise of the 747 and the eager lapping of two tongues.

Berman threw himself into the job with total dedication. Here he was, kneeling at the feet of the desirably, dangerously dominant woman of all his fantasies. She was letting him prove himself! Prove he could suck pussy better than some inexperienced little flying partygirl! He sucked and slobbered at Moira in a frenzy. His jaw worked insistently, his tongue thrust in and out of her cunt, his lips worried at her clit. He grabbed her hips in his hands and pulled her toward his face. Moira giggled with delight. To urge him on she grabbed his ears and yanked them savagely. The sudden pain threw Berman into little ecstasies. He groaned and redoubled his efforts.

Abigail was using a more genteel approach. She caressed the soft, soft skin at the back of Sharon's slender neck, and she moved her hips gently up and down, rubbing her pussy lightly across Sharon's delicate mouth as the girl worked on Abigail's clitoris with a series of subtle, fleeting caresses with the tip of her tongue.

Abigail felt her flesh tingle and glow, felt the desire blossom, and knew this wasn't going to take long. Sharon was licking her so sweetly and knowingly. The girl's tongue flicked up and down like a butterfly's wing, and somehow the lighter the caresses were, the more they turned Abigail on. She began panting with expectation. This was going to be no contest!

But at that moment the plane hit an air pocket. The floor lurched.

There was a soft musical chime.

"Ladies and gentlemen," a voice came over the intercom. "The captain has turned on the seat-belt sign. Please return to your seats at once, and make sure your seat belts are securely fastened."

"No!" Moira complained as Berman started to get up off the floor. "What the hell are you doing? Don't stop, you dummy! Not now!"

The plane dipped and bounced through another air pocket. "But I feel sick," Berman moaned.

"Want me to go on?" Sharon whispered to Abigail.

"Oh, yes! Yes, yes, yes!" Abigail told the girl, urging her mouth back between her thighs.

"Get back down there on the floor and suck my twat, you fat jerk!" Moira snapped at Berman. "Abigail's gaining on me!"

"But—" The rest of his protest was smothered as Moira grabbed hold of him by the hair at the back of his head and forced his face against her crotch. She swung her hips from side to side, and rubbed herself angrily across Berman's mouth.

Again the plane sank and lurched through air turbulence.

Abigail shut her eyes and ignored it, and made herself ignore, also, Moira's muttered curses and Berman's smothered complaints and slobbering noises. Abigail was determined to come. She tried to think of a truly exciting fantasy, to help her up and over the edge into orgasm. A familiar face came into her imagination immediately— James Barrington's face.

The plane lurched again. But Abigail was no longer aware of it. She gasped as Sharon's agile tongue fluttered up and down between her labia. And then Sharon closed her lips on Abigail's clit and sucked and tongued it with dedicated fervor.

Abigail clenched her fists and arched her back and sobbed as she reached orgasm. She caressed Sharon's soft hair. She sighed as Sharon slowed her mouth movements and licked her languorously till her climax gradually subsided.

"You faked it!" Moira cried in fury.

"Didn't," murmured Abigail, with a slow smile of satisfaction. And something about her tone made it obvious she was telling the truth.

"Hermie, you failed me!" Moira wailed, realizing she must admit defeat. "You useless, stupid—"

"I'm gonna throw up!" he told her, finally managing to free his face from her twat. "Jesus, I'm gonna—"

"Here, Mr. Berman!" said Sharon. Suddenly she was a stewardess again. She grabbed a sick-bag from the pocket in one of the seats and pushed it toward Berman.

Not a moment too soon. He coughed and retched and vomited noisily into the bag, with great heavings of his shoulders and gut.

"My god, why am I always surrounded by incompetents?" Moira moaned. "Why, why, why? First George, and now this. Oh, it's not fair! It's not, not fair!"

"Don't let it get to you, Moira," said Abigail, deliberately sounding as condescending as possible. "Why, I'm sure it can't be your fault."

Meanwhile, the turbulence and the seat-belt announcement had awakened some of the other passengers. "Stewardess!" someone called—the elderly lady sitting at the back. "Stewardess, what's going on?" She reached for her seat belt, and discovered Abigail's panties lying in her lap. She peered at them in the dim cabin lighting, then groped for her glasses.

"I've got to go," Sharon said. She bent and kissed Abigail on the mouth, and Abigail tasted her own juices on Sharon's lips.

"Stewardess! Whatever is this?" The old lady was holding the panties up and sniffing at them.

"Explain that if you can," Abigail murmured to Sharon.

"No problem," said Sharon. She squeezed Abigail's shoulder. "Thanks for the great time."

Then she stood up and straightened her uniform and went over to the old lady. "I'm sorry, madam," she said in her best professional voice. "We found that underwear in one of the toilets, and thought it might be yours."

Abigail didn't stick around to hear the rest of it. She said good night to Moira, and to Herman Berman, who was still puking his guts out. She walked to the front row of seats, where George and Brad had retreated.

She found George awake and Brad asleep.

"Had enough fun back there?" said George, his voice weary and sour.

Abigail sat down beside him. She didn't bother to answer the question. "What happened with him?" she said, gesturing at Brad.

"He gave me a little lecture on the importance of sleep in an actor's career. Then he put in his genuine Flent wax earplugs, ate some Maalox tablets, loosened his shoelaces and his belt, got a couple of pillows and a blanket, and passed right out."

"It figures," said Abigail. "For someone who isn't really a flake, Brad does good imitations." She lapsed into silence. The image of James Barrington that she'd conjured up just before her orgasm was still haunting her.

"Want to tell me what's really on your mind?" asked George.

Abigail sighed. Drink and drugs hadn't really helped during the past couple of days. Maybe telling someone would do some good.

And, so quietly and calmly, she told George all about Lord James Barrington, and how she had become hopelessly infatuated with the man without even knowing why.

George listened carefully through the whole thing. "So have an affair with him," he commented at the end of her monologue. "You're going to be in England. It's perfect. This is your chance to get him out of your system."

Abigail shook her head. "I don't like being the 'other woman' with a married guy. Not when I really want him. And anyway—" She glanced at Brad again, to make sure he was still asleep. "Anyway, there'd be too much risk of Brad finding out. And that would really screw up our relationship. Which I cannot afford to do, because we have to make a movie together. Work comes first, George. This is a great deal Moira's made for me. It hurts me to admit it, but it's true. I'm not going to do anything to screw up this movie."

George nodded slowly. "I see," he said thoughtfully. "Yes, I see. . . ."

Chapter Twelve

Flashbulbs were flashing. Glaring TV lights came to life and shone square into Abigail's face. There was a mob of people. "Miss van Pelt! Independent Television News, Miss van Pelt! Do you have a moment?"

Abigail tried to shield her eyes from the lights. Her head was throbbing. Her stomach was churning. She felt as if she were going to keel over.

"Is it true that you're replacing actress Helen Hingley in the movie *Some Sweet Summer*?" asked an eager young interviewer, thrusting his microphone toward her.

"Tha's right," Abigail mumbled, swaying unsteadily. She grabbed Brad's arm for support.

"What's the shooting schedule?" asked another voice from somewhere behind the lights.

"Is there any truth to the rumor—" another voice cut in.

"All right, that's enough!" said Moira, stepping in front of Abigail. "We've just come off a ten-hour flight. There's time for interviews later. Right now we're going to get some rest."

She grabbed Abigail and hustled her through the press of people, with Brad striding alongside and Herman Berman and George following behind.

"Yay! Yay! Abigail!" screamed a trio of teenagers,

holding signs that said: WELCOME, ABIGAIL—FROM YOUR LONDON FAN CLUB.

"Cut it out!" Herman Berman snarled at them, pressing both hands to his forehead and grimacing in agony.

A little later the five of them were riding in the back of a Daimler limousine from Heathrow into London. "You might have warned us, Herman," Moira was complaining, "that you'd arranged that little reception committee."

"Forgot all about it," Berman muttered, slumping down with his eyes shut. He belched and groaned softly. "All I did was tell the people at the studio which flight we'd be on, and how we'd appreciate someone to meet us. . . ."

"I thought it was excellent," Brad interrupted. He was fresh-faced and bright-eyed, and had even shaved before getting off the plane. "I'm all in favor of whatever publicity we can get, Mr. Berman, speaking personally. It's just a pity that some of us," he glanced at Abigail, "were in no condition to take advantage of the opportunity."

"If you don't shut the fuck up, I'll kill you," Abigail told him in a matter-of-fact monotone. She glanced out of the window and winced. "Why the hell does it have to be so bright outside?"

"It's the time difference," Brad explained, taking her question seriously. "We've gained ten hours. Your biological clock thinks it's nine o'clock at night, but actually the local time is seven in the morning." He stopped, noticing the way that Abigail, Moira, and Berman were all glowering at him. "Sorry," he said meekly.

"You got time to grab some sleep, anyhow, Abby," Berman told her. "The talk-show spot isn't scheduled till eight-thirty tonight. Do whatever you want till then."

"Wonderful," said Abigail. She reflected that there was one advantage in feeling so wrecked and hung over: it made it impossible for her to feel melancholy about James Barrington. All she could think about was how terrible she felt.

Half an hour later, the van Pelt party checked into the Ritz on Piccadilly. Herman Berman took one of the penthouse suites; Abigail and Brad selected a double room on the third floor overlooking Green Park; and Moira and George took a room adjoining.

The hotel was wonderfully quiet. A faint murmur of traffic noise filtered through the open windows, where white gauze curtains billowed gently in the breeze. Outside somewhere, London sparrows were singing. The bed was large and soft. The furnishings were genuine antiques. An Indian carpet covered the floor; there was a functioning marble fireplace; the high ceiling was embellished with ornate plaster moldings. Abigail flopped onto her back on the bed, fully dressed. She closed her eyes.

"Abigail," said Brad, as he carefully unpacked his suitcase and stacked his clothes in the drawers of a bow-fronted bureau. "Look, about this talk show you're going to be doing tonight."

She carefully eased one shoe off and dropped it onto the floor, and then the other. "Hmm?" she murmured.

"Are you sure there's no way I can get on the show with you?" Brad continued. "Just a walk-on spot—"

Abigail groaned. "Brad, we discussed this before we ever left LA. We were lucky that one of the earlier guests canceled out of the show. Else I wouldn't be on it myself. There's no way we can get you on as well."

"I was just thinking," he persisted, "that I could come to the studio with you, and you could just happen to mention to the host that I'm there, and—"

Abigail sat up suddenly. "Enough!" she shouted. "Let me sleep! Go see the sights or something! The Tower of London! Buckingham Palace! The Changing of the Guard! Go see it, anything, just let me sleep!"

Brad hesitated, holding an armful of brown socks. "But I don't know my way around. I've never been here before."

"George'll show you," Abigail improvised, subsiding back onto the bed. "Go get George to play tour-guide.

And don't come back for at least four hours. Get it? No, make that six hours. Understood?"

"I wish I knew why you're acting like this," Brad said, looking hurt.

Abigail seized a pillow and pulled it over her head.

She lay on the bed and waited.

After a few minutes she peeked out from under the pillow; Brad was gone.

Abigail got up, took off her dress and underwear, fell back into bed, and fell asleep.

She woke a little while later, not sure how much time had passed. But most of the aftereffects of the booze and drugs had worn off. Her piercing headache had faded, and her stomach was no longer churning.

A strange sound had awakened her. A rhythmic slap, slap, slap, like a loose window shade flapping in the wind.

Abigail sat up in bed and listened. For a moment there was silence . . . and then she heard the noise again.

Noticing that the connecting door between her room and Moira's room was open, and that the noise seemed to be coming from there, Abigail slipped out of bed. She went to one of her suitcases and rummaged inside, trying to dig out her robe. But she couldn't find it. And so, naked, she crept to the connecting door to Moira's room, and peeked inside.

Herman Berman was stretched out facedown, full-length upon a long, low, Louis XV coffee table in front of the fireplace. He was stark naked. Moira was standing over him, dressed in a laced-up leather tunic that revealed most of her bulging breasts, plus skintight leather breeches, and black-leather boots with five-inch spike heels. She was holding her notebook in one hand and a long-handled lash in the other.

"And then, when I arrived at your mansion yesterday to have a strictly business discussion with you," she was saying, reading from the notebook, "you had the nerve to grab my left boob. I warned you at the time that I would have to punish you for this kind of disgusting behavior. In response you said, and I quote, 'Suck my dick, Moira baby.' Am I correct, Hermie? Isn't that what you said?"

"Yes," he mumbled, craning his neck around to stare up at her apprehensively. "But it was like a manner of speech, Moira. Like, I mean, I didn't mean nothing bad by it. I—"

"Quiet!" she commanded him. "For your disgraceful behavior, which I have just described, you will receive ten more lashes."

"Not ten!" he begged her. "Five, make it five—"

"And an extra two for interrupting me without permission!" Moira exclaimed.

Berman groaned with a mixture of despair and anticipation.

Moira raised the lash and brought it swinging down. Its several leather tails thwacked across Herman's bottom. She raised the lash and brought it down again, and again, in a steady rhythm. Slap, slap, slap—that was the noise that had awakened Abigail just now.

Berman's plump, pale flesh jumped under each blow. Pink marks blossomed. The whole of his ass was turning bright red.

Abigail watched from the doorway with wide-eyed fascination. She'd always known about Berman's submissive fantasies, even though she'd never had the inclination to fulfill them for him herself.

Moira finished beating him and set the lash aside. She was breathing hard from the exertion. She sat down on the end of the bed to rest for a moment.

"Is that it? Can I go now?" Berman asked her.

"Certainly not!" she snapped.

"But I gotta go to the bathroom," he complained in a whining small-boy voice.

Moira laughed scornfully. "You think I'm going to fall for that? No, you've got a lot more punishment yet, Hermie. Why, there are two more whole pages of my notebook, full of your undisciplined, disgraceful conduct!"

"No," said Berman. "No, no, no! I won't let you hit me any more, so there." His voice sounded just like a schoolboy's. He pouted at Moira and then started to get up off the table.

"Why, you disobedient little turd!" she cried. She stepped quickly forward and grabbed his ear. "You will get back on that table this minute!"

"I won't I won't I won't!" Berman hollered. "Leggo my ear! Ow! Ow!"

"Get back on there!" Moira jabbed him with the toe of her boot, then dug its spike heel into his raw-red ass.

Berman whined and cringed from her. Bit by bit she forced him back into his submissive position stretched out facedown on the table.

Abigail saw that one reason he was reluctant to stay there was that he had a huge erection. His big, hard cock was sandwiched between his body and the antique polished wood.

Moira stood over him, breathing hard. She kept her boot planted in the small of his back, holding him down like a hunter with a trophy. "I'm going to have to get a lot more strict with you, Herman," she told him. "A lot more. I can see I've been letting you off far, far too easily."

"Ow!" he complained. "Get your foot off my back!"

"How dare you talk to me like that!" She reached for the lash and thwacked it across his ass a couple more times. "I am Mistress Moira to you, Hermie, and you will not speak to me without permission! You will not!" And she thwacked him again.

Berman squirmed under her. He gulped and gasped. He was very near orgasm. But he kept struggling to resist Moira—struggling seemed to turn him on.

"I'm going to stop your wriggling, once and for all," Moira told him. "I'm going to have to tie you up, Hermie." She glanced around, looking for something suitable.

And at that moment she noticed Abigail peering into the room through the connecting door.

"Why, Abigail," Moira said, her mouth dropping open.

"Hey, I'm sorry," Abigail apologized. "The door was open and I heard the noises and I couldn't help—"

"That's quite all right, my dear," said Moira, instantly recovering her composure. "There's no need to apologize. And please, don't go. Come in, come in! Come join us! You're just the person I need to help me with my little problem here!"

Chapter Thirteen

Abigail hesitated. The last thing she'd ever expected to do was participate in one of her weirdo sister's kinky sex scenes. As far as Abigail was concerned, Moira's taste for female dominance was a freaky aberration that Abigail didn't share to the slightest degree.

On the other hand, though, it was hard simply to turn around and walk out. There was Herman Berman, his fat flesh draped over an antique French coffee table in the sumptuous luxury of the London Ritz. And there was Moira, her stiletto-heeled boot planted in the middle of Berman's back, her breasts almost falling out of the laced-up leather bodice of her dominatrix outfit, her face flushed with the exertion of controlling her disobedient 200-pound sex-slave.

Abigail licked her lips. "What exactly do you want me to do, Moira?" she asked tentatively.

"Find something to truss him up with. Damn it, I'm sure I told George to pack my nylon rope. I'll bet he left it out of my suitcase on purpose!"

"Where is George, incidentally?" Abigail asked, taking a cautious step into the room.

"He went to see the sights with Brad. Which was your idea, as I understand it. And that was fine by me. I told George to do some shopping for me while he was out. I need a new riding crop, and the British crops are by far the best— Stop struggling, you!" she snapped at Berman as he began wriggling more violently under her boot.

"We could tie him up with panty hose," Abigail suggested. She circled around Berman. She bent down and peered into his face. "If that's all right with you, Herman."

Moira gasped in disbelief. "If it's all right with him? My god, Abigail, you don't know the first thing about this, do you? We do whatever we want, my dear! Hermie has no say at all in the matter. Why, if we choose to tie him up and tickle his balls with a feather for a few hours, we don't need to ask his permission. We do whatever we want to. Right, Hermie?" She prodded his ass with the handle of her lash.

"Uh," said Berman.

"You see?" said Moira. "He understands. So get the panty hose, Abigail, by all means. And we'll tie him to the bed."

"But Moira," Berman started complaining again, "I ain't kidding. I really got to go to the bathroom!"

Moira threw her head back and laughed. "Later, Hermie, later. Abigail, you'll find lots of panty hose in that suitcase over there."

Abigail went to where Moira had indicated. She found the necessary items. "Maybe I should go and put some clothes on," she said, feeling self-conscious about her nakedness.

"Why bother, my dear?" said Moira. "I'll be naked too, soon enough. And then you'd be the odd one out. Help me drag him over to the bed now."

Abigail went to the other side of Berman. Hesitantly, she took hold of his arm.

"What are you going to do?" he whined to Moira. "Hey, I'll be good, all right? I know I've been a bad boy, but I'll be good in future. I promise! Cross my heart! Honest Injun!"

Moira lifted her boot from the middle of his back and helped him stand up. "I'm sorry, Hermie," she told him, "but I really don't believe a word of it."

108

"No, no, it's true!" he said, cringing from her.

"Now, you be good and come along with me," she insisted. She grabbed his wrist and expertly doubled his arm up behind his back.

"Ow! No! Let go!" he complained.

"Tut, tut. So much noise. Come on, you!" And she expertly frog-marched him to the bed.

Herman fell forward onto it. Moira flipped him over and quickly lashed his left wrist to one of the posts of the old-fashioned headboard. "Tie his other wrist," she told Abigail.

Abigail smiled uncertainly at Berman and took hold of his pudgy wrist. He disconcerted her by looking up at her plaintively. Then, deliberately, he winked.

Abigail decided that if she stopped and thought about this scene, it would seem so ridiculous she'd never go through with it. So she hauled Berman's arm as far toward the corner of the bed as she could, quickly knotted one end of some panty hose to the headboard, then tied it to Berman's wrist, avoiding looking him in the eye again.

"That's good," said Moira, tying each of Berman's ankles to the foot of the bed so he was lying spread-eagled on his back. His cock stood up huge and throbbing. His chest rose and fell as he took deep breaths. He squirmed in his bonds. "You tied 'em awful tight," he whined.

Moira jumped onto the bed and swung her leg over him so she was kneeling on either side of his chest. She slapped him warningly on the cheek. "Now, Hermie, haven't I told you about speaking without my permission?"

Berman didn't answer. He pouted.

"Haven't I told you?" Moira repeated. She grabbed some of the hair on his chest and tugged sharply. "Haven't I?"

"Yes," Berman muttered.

"Yes, Mistress Moira!" She reached lower and carefully took hold of Berman's balls.

"Yes, Mistress Moira!" Berman quickly repeated after her, a look of sudden anxiety in his eyes—mixed, at the same time, with guilty excitement.

Moira turned to Abigail, who was standing a couple of paces back from the bed. "You see, my dear," said Moira, "the old saying is perfectly true. When you've got 'em by the balls, their hearts and minds will follow." Again, carefully, she slid her fingers under Herman's balls and cupped them almost lovingly. "Right, Hermie?"

"Yes, Mistress Moira!"

Moira laughed with delight. "But we still have to punish you, don't we, you bad boy? For talking out of turn and causing me so much trouble. Let's see, now. Abigail, why don't you go and tickle the soles of his feet?"

"Oh, no!" Berman squealed. "Anything but that!"

"Pay no attention to him," said Moira. "Just do it."

Hesitantly Abigail walked to the bottom of the bed and trailed her fingernails along the sole of Berman's left foot. He squirmed and tried to pull away from her.

"Oh no!" he cried. "Oh please. Moira. I'll be good! Please! I promise!"

"More," Moira said to Abigail.

Abigail shook her head. She knew, intellectually, that Berman was getting off on this whole scene. Still, she couldn't stop herself from feeling sorry for him. Instinctively she wanted to release him. "I'm sorry, Moira, I don't think I can do it," she confessed.

"Well, if you can't, I certainly can, my dear," said Moira. She got off Berman and walked around to where Abigail was already standing at the bottom of the bed.

Moira reached down and started tickling Berman's foot. For a moment nothing happened. Then, suddenly he made little falsetto whimpering noises and started squirming from side to side in terrible agitation.

"Now, Hermie," Moira said, delicately tracing her fingernails along the outline of his instep, "you really are going to try harder to be good, in the future. Aren't you, dear?"

110

"Yes, yes! I'll be good! Oooh, stop it, stop it!"

"He loves every minute, you know," Moira murmured in Abigail's ear. "Don't let him fool you."

"If you say so," Abigail replied dubiously.

"And you'll do whatever I tell you, won't you, Hermie?" Moira went on, turning her attention back to her captive and tickling him more.

"Yes, yes! I'll do whatever you say! Oooh! Ah! Please! I can't stand it!"

"Stop your complaining," Moira told him. "You deserve every minute of this after the way you've been behaving, today and last night. Speaking of which, I never did punish you for the way you disappointed me, when you were eating my pussy on the plane."

"But—but I couldn't help that," Berman complained. "I was airsick."

"Maybe so, but even before you got sick, your performance was still pathetic." Moira paused thoughtfully. "I do believe you need some practice, Hermie. And I've just realized, this is the perfect opportunity."

Moira turned to her sister. "Abigail, dear, how would you like to sit on his face? I'll stay here and make sure he pleases you properly." There was a malevolent gleam in her eye.

Abigail wasn't sure she really wanted to have Berman licking her clit. On the other hand, she'd deliberately walked into this scene. And there was still the temptation to see exactly what Moira would do.

"All right," she agreed reluctantly. She went and kneeled just above Berman's head, facing the bottom of the bed, with her back to its headboard.

"Put one knee at each side of his shoulders," said Moira, "and lower yourself onto him. Keep your legs spread wide apart, else he won't be able to push his little tongue up inside. Isn't that right, Hermie?" Once again Moira scrabbled her fingernails tantalizingly over the sole of Berman's foot.

His body jerked and twitched, but his response was

111

muffled. Abigail had already sat down on his face. She felt his lips searching between her labia. Then his tongue crept up and into her, and he started licking busily.

"Is he doing it properly?" Moira asked.

Abigail rocked gently and fro. Then she leaned forward and braced herself by placing the palms of her hands on Berman's chest. She lifted her crotch just a little way away from his face, so he could breathe. His tongue stretched up and lapped her in a steady rhythm.

"He's doing fine," said Abigail.

"As well as your little stewardess friend did it last night?" Moira asked skeptically.

"Uh . . . not quite that well," Abigail had to admit.

"Then, try harder!" Moira snapped at Berman. She started tickling him again. "I'm going to keep doing this to you till you please Abigail properly and completely. In fact— In fact I won't stop tickling you till you make her come!"

As Moira spoke, a look of sexual excitement showed on her face—excitement at the prospect of what she was about to do to him.

Berman moaned and wriggled, but there was no way he could escape. Moira commenced tickling his feet and continued to do so mercilessly—first one, then the other, lightly and tantalizingly, with just the edge of her fingernails.

At the same time, she thrust her other hand between her own legs and started masturbating. She half closed her eyes and took quick, shallow breaths through her slightly parted lips.

She focused on Berman licking Abigail's clit. He was gasping and straining, sweating and grunting. His tongue was working on her frantically while his body twisted and writhed in its bonds, tormented by Moira's relentless tickling.

Meanwhile Abigail had closed her eyes to concentrate on what his tongue was doing to her. The more Moira tickled him, the more desperately he licked Abigail's clit. His tongue moved furiously up and down, to and fro.

In fact he was getting so desperate, he no longer knew what he was doing. Half the time, his tongue either missed Abigail's clitoris altogether, or jammed against it too hard. Abigail realized she wasn't going to be able to come.

He was so out of his mind with the tickling he couldn't concentrate on pleasing her.

But Moira was on the edge of orgasm. She was panting, her breasts heaving and almost spilling out of the laced-up bodice of her costume.

Her left hand moved busily between her thighs, bringing herself to her climax. Her right hand continued mercilessly working on the soles of Berman's feet. On and on she tickled him, and each time he writhed and jerked helplessly it just turned her on more.

Finally the excitement was too much for Moira. She closed her eyes and gave a little moan as she climaxed. She swayed, steadied herself against the bed, and shivered as the orgasm rippled through her.

Abigail saw what was happening and decided she had to put Berman out of his misery. And the only way to do that was by faking an orgasm. So she gave a little cry, jammed her hips down onto Berman's face, and wriggled from side to side. Then she gasped.

She wasn't accustomed to faking orgasm, so she wasn't sure if she'd done a good job. But since Moira was only just coming out of her own climax, she probably wouldn't notice.

Abigail lifted herself off Berman and slid off the bed. Moira sat down heavily on the end of the bed, breathing hard. Berman, still tied hand and foot, lay on his back with his eyes closed. His face was bright red, and his mouth glistened wet with Abigail's juices. He was gasping and groaning.

"Well, Abigail, dear," said Moira, with her thin, supercilious smile. She parted a stray strand of hair into place. "Wasn't that nice?"

"It was fine," Abigail said, glancing nervously at Berman.

"Don't you just love having a man straining to satisfy your every whim?" said Moira, with a dreamy look in her eyes.

"I guess," said Abigail. She wanted to say more, but she knew it wasn't worth debating sex with her sister.

Moira wasn't really listening, anyway. "The thing is," she went on, reaching out and grabbing Berman's big fat cock, "Hermie loves it too. Don't you, dear?"

Flat on his back, with his eyes still closed, Berman nodded feebly.

"He knows he deserves to be punished. He knows what a naughty, naughty boy he's been. All the lies he's told, all the women he's ever deceived and taken advantage of —isn't that right, Hermie?—and the crooked business deals, and the rotten, sordid exploitation enterprises." Moira played with Berman's cock, running her fingers up and down it, tickling it, tantalizing him. "That's why he really needs to be punished," Moira went on. "Am I right, Hermie?"

Berman turned his face away. Again, wordlessly, he nodded.

"Well," Abigail said, feeling embarrassed and out of place, "I think I'd better—"

"Aren't you going to stay and help me humiliate him some more?" said Moira. "My god, Abigail, you're such a little prude. I really thought you wanted to be friendly toward me for a change."

"Friendly, sure," said Abigail. "But— I mean, this just isn't my scene." Secretly she wanted to go and masturbate. Berman's oral ministrations had turned her on halfway; she needed to complete the job.

"Anyway," she improvised, "I expect Brad will be back soon, and I don't want him to find me—"

"Brad and George won't be back for hours," Moira interrupted, continuing to caress Berman's dick while he moaned softly and squirmed in his bonds. "But if you want to leave, Abigail, you go right ahead. I must warn you, though, you'll be missing something very special."

Abigail stopped, despite herself. "What's that?" she said, unable to contain her curiosity.

"I'm going to give Hermie, here, his enema," said Moira, with a wicked smile.

Berman suddenly seemed to regain his senses. "A what?" he muttered. He craned his head up and opened his eyes. "A what?"

"Well, you kept complaining that you wanted to go to the bathroom," Moira told him. She let go of Berman's cock and walked to her suitcase. She reached inside and pulled out an enema bag with a long rubber tube attached. "This is what happens to small boys who need toilet training."

"Uh," Berman grunted. His eyes fixed on the enema bag. He swallowed hard. Obviously the idea was even more of a turn-on for him than being spanked and tickled had been.

Moira turned to Abigail. "Why don't you grease the nozzle dear, and push it in while I go and run some hot water?"

Abigail backed away. "Not me," she said. "Thanks, but no thanks."

Moira scowled. "Oh, all right. I suppose if I want this done properly, I'll just have to do it myself."

"See you later, Herman," Abigail called to the plump figure on the bed.

Berman didn't answer. He didn't even seem to hear her. He was still staring with guilty excitement at the enema bag, and seemed aware of nothing else.

Chapter Fourteen

Abigail returned to her own room and closed the connecting door from Moira's room securely behind her. She leaned against the door panels and shut her eyes for a moment. She took several deep breaths and shook her head, as if to get rid of all the weirdness.

Enemas, yet!

Then she walked across to her suitcases. Brad had put his things away, but her clothes were still packed. She had to get organized.

She wasn't even sure what time it was. She had to check her schedule of meetings and rehearsals for the next few days, she had to figure out what to wear and what to say in the talk-show appearance she was supposed to make later that evening. . . .

As she opened the first of her suitcases, someone knocked on the door of her room.

Her first thought was that it must be Brad, back from his tour around town. "It's not locked," she called.

She heard the door open. She looked up.

It wasn't Brad standing there. It was Lord James Barrington.

Abigail stood up slowly, feeling totally disoriented and stunned. Then, abruptly she realized she was still naked. She grabbed a dress out of the suitcase and quickly held it up in front of her body.

"What the hell," she said slowly and in disbelief, "are you doing here?"

Lord Barrington closed the door behind him and stood there looking at her with an amused look on his face.

Abigail shook her head. "No," she said. "This is all too much. I can't deal with this." She went and sat on the edge of the bed. She was still stupidly holding the dress in front of her. "How did you know I was in the country? How did you—"

"I had to see you, Abigail," he said softly. "I knew you were in London because I'm in the habit of watching a morning news program while I eat breakfast. *Around and About,* the daily guide to what's happening and who's appearing in London. They showed you arriving at Heathrow Airport. To work on a new film, I understand."

Abigail looked at him, then away from him. She didn't know whether she wanted to set her eyes on him or not.

"I thought I made it clear I never wanted to see you again," she snapped.

Lord Barrington smiled as if she had said something that faintly amused him. "I gather you're still annoyed with me for being married," he told her.

She glared at him. "Do you have to be so damned supercilious?"

He shook his head. "Not at all. But I do find it hard to take your anger seriously." He walked into the room. He glanced around at the furniture and the decor, and went to the window. "Very nice, very elegant," he said. "Much more pleasant than my room at the Beverly Wilshire. Wouldn't you agree?"

Abigail closed her eyes and summoned her strength. Then she stood up. "Listen," she said, "I don't know how you found out where I'm staying—"

"The film studios, of course," Lord Barrington told her, turning away from the view out of the window. "I had my secretary phone them from the House of Lords."

Abigail gathered her strength yet again. "All right. As I was saying, I told you how I feel about this when we were in Los Angeles. I don't have affairs with married men. Ever. Period. You're a great guy—and a great lover, and I like you, but I'm not going to be woman number two. Maybe it's pride. I don't know, I don't care. I just want you out of here. Else you're going to fuck up my life."

Her voice was rising in pitch and she felt all her muscles tensing.

By contrast Lord Barrington seemed totally relaxed and at ease. He smiled fondly at Abigail, as if she were his favorite daughter throwing an adolescent tantrum over nothing that was really important. He put his hands in the pockets of his blue pinstripe pants and looked at her with his head tilted to one side. "You're just as I remembered you, you know," he told her.

"Goddamn it!" Abigail shouted, losing all her self-control. "I'm telling you, James Barrington, stop patronizing me! I want you the hell out of here!"

He stepped quickly toward her, as if all he'd been waiting for, all along, was for her to lose her cool. She tried to back away from him, but the bed was behind her, and before she could step around it he suddenly reached out and grabbed the dress she was holding in front of her body.

He ripped it out of her hands and threw it aside.

His face was grim now. His attention was focused totally on her, and for the first time she felt scared of him. He seemed so deliberate, so powerful and determined.

He took her face between his hands. She seized his wrists and tried to pull his hands away from her, but he was stronger than she was. He held her face and brought his mouth down to hers.

Abigail raised her knee and jammed it into his stomach.

Lord Barrington grunted, perhaps in pain, perhaps merely in surprise—she couldn't tell. He didn't let go of her.

She twisted and struggled and finally freed herself. She

was breathing hard, her pulse beating fast. She wondered what the hell she should do. "My sister's in the next room," she said. "I'll call her in here, through the connecting door, and—"

Abigail broke off, suddenly remembering what was undoubtedly going on in Moira's room at that very moment. Herman Berman, big-time movie producer, tied to the bed with nylon panty hose, while Moira van Pelt, prominent Hollywood movie agent, dressed in skintight black leather, shoved an enema tube up his ass and beat his quivering white flesh with a multithonged lash.

"You'll call your sister, and—?" Lord Barrington said, mocking her. He moved toward her again. He could see her indecision and her repressed desire for him. There was no **dou**bt in his mind that he was going to claim her and have her.

"Goddamn you," Abigail said, clenching her fists. "Why can't you leave me alone? I've told you how I feel—"

"You're being irrational, my dear Abigail." He reached out with surprising speed and grabbed her wrist. His grip was rigid and almost painfully strong. He started dragging her toward him. "You would have screamed for help long before now if you really didn't want this," he said. "The force of attraction between us is so strong. I feel it myself, for heaven's sake. I've told you that my wife has no interest in what I do in my personal, private life."

He paused, struggling with Abigail all the time. She had tried to pry his fingers off her with her left hand; he simply grabbed her left wrist too. Then she tried to bite his fingers; he lifted his arm up and away. He forced her back toward the bed.

"I only mentioned my wife because I felt I should be totally frank with you," he said. "Because I care for you considerably, Abigail. Damn it, will you listen to me?"

He pushed her suddenly, and she fell backward onto the bed.

He fell down on top of her, his three-piece suit against her naked body. She writhed and struggled. He gasped

120

and grunted, got a hold on one of her wrists and twisted her arm.

Abigail cried out in sudden pain. She turned on her side to relieve the pressure at her shoulder. Lord Barrington twisted her arm more, and suddenly she found herself lying flat on her stomach on the bed, unable even to see him, let alone fight back.

"Get off me!" she gasped, simply feeling angry now that he was doing whatever he wanted with her. From the start she'd felt powerless with him—emotionally, and now physically. "All I want is for you to leave me alone," she said, and her voice started to break.

He kept hold of her with one hand, pinning her to the bed. With his other hand he unbuttoned his jacket. He shrugged it off and tossed it aside. Then he got rid of his tie, his waistcoat, and his shirt.

Abigail squirmed and tried to free herself, but each time she struggled he increased the pressure on her arm twisted up behind her, and the pressure made her wince and succumb.

She heard him kick off his shoes, his pants, then his underwear. He was breathing hard. She imagined his cock standing out enormous, stiff, about to violate her body.

Abigail summoned the last of her strength. "This is rape, do you understand me?" she told him, making her voice sound grim and determined. "I'm going to scream rape. If you do this, so help me, Barrington, I'll scream so loud, the whole damn hotel will hear me. How'll you like that kind of publicity? I mean it!"

Lord Barrington didn't reply. He lowered himself onto her, and his cock probed between her thighs. She felt the head of it nudge against the opening of her vagina.

Abigail drew in her breath to scream, but the scream somehow wouldn't form itself in her throat. Helplessly she let the breath out again in a sob. "Damn you!" she cried. With her free hand she clutched at the bed-sheet. "Damn you, you bastard!"

Lord Barrington's breath was hot on the back of her

neck. He sensed the last of her resistance going out of her, and he let go of the arm he had been holding to pin her to the bed. He pushed his knees between hers and forced her legs apart. He slid one arm under her belly and pulled her ass up. With his other hand he felt for her cunt, then guided his cock to it.

"No!" Abigail told him. She clenched her fists and pounded them on the bed. "No, no, no!"

Lord Barrington worked the head of his cock between her labia. He thrust slowly forward and into her.

She was dry—but not entirely. The moistness that had begun to gather inside her was testament to how much she secretly wanted him.

Lord Barrington pushed and pushed again, relentlessly. His cock worked into her, inch by inch. He didn't stop until he was totally embedded in her.

Then he wiggled his hips and worked his cock around inside her, from behind. Already Abigail could feel herself responding, feel the passion growing, feel herself getting wetter inside.

She closed her eyes and cursed herself for being so weak. She never let men treat her like this. Never!

His arms circled her body and hugged her to him. His hands found her breasts and he held them tightly, just the way she remembered. He pinched her nipples, fleetingly at first, then harder, till she gave a little gasp. The pleasure spreading from her groin and the sudden little pulse of pain from her nipples seemed to drain all the strength from her muscles. She subsided under him, opened herself to him. She was unable even to pretend to fight him any more.

Barrington withdrew from her a moment, and turned her on her side. He lay down on his side also, facing her, with his legs between hers. He watched her as he carefully put himself back inside her.

"When I realized that you were in London, it seemed you must have come here for me," he said. He thrust himself in, all the way. His cock was so long, she felt as if she was impaled on him.

"Just coincidence," she muttered, and bit her lip, momentarily overwhelmed by a wave of pure pleasure spreading from her cunt and clitoris to every smallest nerve of her body. "Came here for the movie . . . was determined not to see you—"

James Barrington started fucking her harder, in long, sure strokes. He cupped her chin in his hand and kissed her deliberately on the mouth while he went on fucking her. His tongue probed for hers. Abigail responded; there was no point in fighting him now. She'd spent the last two days trying not to fantasize about him. Now, at least, she could let herself enjoy it with him.

Lord Barrington rolled her onto her back. He braced himself over her and fucked her some more. He looked down at her, studying her beauty. There was a manic intensity about him.

"I want you," he told her. "I want you in every way."

She drew up her knees, to take him in deeper—as deep as he could possibly go inside her.

He grabbed her by the shoulders roughly, and shook her. "I want to possess you," he told her. "I need to have you. I need it, so strongly—" He grunted and paused to stop himself from coming.

"I seem to have gotten hooked on this myself," she told him.

"Do you love me?" he asked her, staring deeply into her eyes.

Abigail quickly shook her head. "No."

Her response seemed to throw him off balance. For the first time, she saw him hesitate. For maybe seconds he was unsure of himself.

But then his grip tightened on her shoulders, and he fucked her even harder than before, pounding into her body as if he wanted to punish her more than pleasure her.

123

He pressed himself close, on top of her, with her legs pulled up, her knees almost at her chin. He circled his arms around her and hugged her in that position so she couldn't move at all. He eased his cock in deeper and deeper, till it hurt a little and she cried out.

He held himself inside her like that and wiggled his hips from side to side. Somehow the bone just above his cock was pressing right against her clitoris—and he seemed to know it.

"Come," he told her, staring into her eyes. "I want you to come now, Abigail."

She tried to move, just to prove that she still had options left. But he had her totally trapped in his powerful arms. And he kept on and on rubbing against her.

"Come!" he told her again, as if issuing some royal edict. "Come, Abigail!"

She swallowed hard and gasped. She clutched at him. She couldn't fight him on any level. He had her, and he knew it. The sensations were building, the tension was growing.

"Come!" he told her. He shook her savagely. "Come!"

And then it hit her. She closed her eyes and trembled and whimpered as the orgasm took momentary control of her body. She gasped; she cried; she subsided in his arms.

Slowly, gradually, Lord Barrington loosened his grip on her. He allowed her to straighten her legs, and he pulled his cock midway out of her. He stroked her hair, then her breasts. His touch was tender now. All the aggression had gone out of him.

He kissed her tenderly. At the same time, he returned to his position on his side, still facing her. He moved his cock in and out, slowly and languorously while he went on kissing her.

Then he drew his head back a little so that he could look at her face. "So very beautiful," he murmured. He caressed her cheek with his fingertips, then ran his hand

124

lower and fondled her breasts, where he had clutched them hard just a little earlier.

He went on fucking her gently. And then without warning, he had his orgasm. Abigail saw the emotion on his face. He closed his eyes for a couple of seconds, and he lay still beside her.

Chapter Fifteen

"I still don't like it," Abigail said.

Lord Barrington raised his eyebrows. "What? Our love-making?"

"No!" She gave him a vexed look. "Will you try to take me seriously, just for a minute?"

Lord Barrington gently disentangled himself from her. "I will try," he said. He kissed her on the forehead, then stood up, still naked. His cock was still half-erect, glistening wet from her cunt.

"I mean you forced me into it, just now," she said.

"Only to the extent that you were reluctant to acknowledge your own desires," he said. He went into the adjoining bathroom, and Abigail had to wait until the water had stopped running before she could talk to him some more.

"All right," she said when Lord Barrington walked back into the bedroom. She sat up in bed. "So I gave in, just now, despite my better judgment. But I still don't like this—this sneaking around. You're cheating on your wife, and I'm doing something with you that my boyfriend, Brad wouldn't like."

Lord Barrington picked up his underwear from the Indian carpet and began to get dressed. "Life, Abigail, is seldom as simple as we would wish," he said philosophically.

"That sounds like a cop-out to me," she told him. "Who

is your wife, anyway? The Countess of Dorset, isn't that what you said?"

"Quite correct." He pulled his trousers on, walked to the mirror inside the door of the built-in closet, and carefully removed lint from his blue pinstripes.

Abigail glared at him. "You're not being very helpful," she complained. Privately she had a sudden fantasy of getting her sister, Moira, to work on Lord James Barrington. Although, she suspected, he would never allow himself to be put in a submissive or helpless position. He was too savvy for that, and too accustomed to having things his own way. That's what made him so damned complacent —and irritating.

He finished picking lint and turned to her with his friendly, indulgent, disarming smile. "I'm sorry, Abigail. I must admit I'm worried about the time. I should be at the House right now. There's a vote due this morning, and my presence will be missed."

"You mean, the House of Lords?" said Abigail.

"Indeed, I mean the House of Lords." He went and picked up his waistcoat and tie.

"Isn't the Lords sort of like the U.S. Senate? They get to approve the stuff that the Congress has done?"

"More or less," said Lord Barrington, carefully tying a double-Windsor knot in his necktie. "Anyway, my dear Abigail, I should be there. Should have been there all morning, but I couldn't resist stopping here to see you."

"What is the time, anyway?" she asked, getting out of bed and walking over to him.

"Almost eleven," he told her.

"Early." Abigail squinted out of the window at the bright sunlight over Green Park. "I thought I'd slept longer. Brad'll be gone for hours, yet."

Lord Barrington glanced at her and raised one eyebrow. "Do you wish to accompany me, Abigail? It's certainly possible. There's a separate visitor's gallery for friends of the peers."

"To the House of Lords? You mean it?"

"Why, certainly. But you'll have to hurry." He smiled condescendingly, amused by her obvious excitement. Her awkward questions about his wife had been swiftly and painlessly diverted by this opportunity to observe British aristocracy in action.

"Of course I've been to London before," Abigail told him in a taxi a short while later. "But you're the first real live lord I've ever met. Let alone royal relative."

The taxi turned left at Hyde Park Corner and started down toward Buckingham Palace.

"See the flag on top of the palace?" Lord Barrington pointed it out to Abigail. "The Union Jack. That indicates that the Queen is in residence."

"As opposed to what?" said Abigail, looking out at the grand building behind its tall railings. Two guards in scarlet uniforms and bearskins were marching across the courtyard. Tourists were lined up at the railings, snapping pictures.

"Well, Her Majesty often stays at Windsor Castle, or up in Balmoral," said Lord Barrington. "Anyway, she is at home here, today. How would you like to drop in on her some time in the next few weeks, Abigail?"

Abigail turned and stared at him. "Are you kidding?"

Lord Barrington shrugged. "It could be arranged. After all, I am one of the family."

Abigail sat back in her seat and stared at him. "You're too much," she said. "I guess I can see why I had a hard time getting you off my mind the last couple of days."

"You did?" He looked at her suspiciously, as if unsure whether to believe that she was actually saying something complimentary to him.

"Sure did," she answered.

"Well, you have been in my thoughts also," he said. He covered her hand with his and squeezed gently. Then, on impulse, he drew her to him and kissed her on the mouth.

"Oh shit," Abigail said as he released her but con-

129

tinued to stare romantically into her eyes. "Brad wouldn't like this. I don't know what the hell I'm going to do, James. I mean, I have to make a movie with the guy during the next two months."

Lord Barrington placed his forefinger upon Abigail's lips. "Let us discuss such things later," he said. "Today, at least, we can—how do you say it, in America? Play hockey?"

"*Hooky,*" Abigail corrected him. "Hell, all right. So where's this House of Lords, anyhow?"

"It's attached to that large tower with a clock on top," said Lord Barrington, with deadpan humor. "Big Ben, over there, the other side of the square. Perhaps you've seen pictures of it on post cards?"

Meanwhile, back at the Ritz, Herman Berman was just emerging from a lengthy spell in the bathroom. "Jesus, Moira," he said, with a rueful expression. "The things you do to a guy."

She was sitting on the end of the bed, still wearing her dominatrix costume. While waiting for Berman to recover from the effects of the enema she had forced upon him, she had started idly buffing her nails.

"Not complaining, I trust, Hermie," she said archly.

Berman shook his head. "No way. You were right, honey. I needed some of the old B&D. I needed all of it, all the way."

"Hermie," said Moira, "you should understand one thing. You do not call me 'honey.' " She put away her nail file and clasped her hands on her knee. She gave him her professional, frosty smile.

Berman adjusted his jockey shorts and went and found his clothes.

"Sorry, Moira," he said, giving her an uneasy grin, as if he wasn't exactly sure to what extent they were still playing their fantasy roles. He started getting dressed.

"You know," he went on, "You and me should've gotten hooked up a long while back." He buckled his belt across his ample belly. "I could've done you a lot of favors in this business."

"I've managed quite well on my own, my dear," Moira pointed out.

Berman gestured dismissively. "I could've made you the biggest agent in Hollywood by now." He pulled his shirt on and started buttoning it.

Moira frowned. "Hermie, I get the distinct impression you have something on your mind. Something you want to say to me. Why not come right out with it?"

Berman fumbled with his gold cufflinks. He was silent for a long moment. Then, awkwardly, he came and sat down next to Moira on the bed. "Honey—uh, I mean, Moira—" He reached out tentatively, as if he half expected her to slap his wrist. He laid his hand on her arm.

"Yes?" said Moira, again with the frosty smile.

"You ever considered getting married?" Berman blurted out.

Moira showed no sign of surprise. She reached out and patted Berman on the cheek.

"Hermie, you are a dear, dear man," she said, "all the more so because you know how to submit to a superior, exceptional woman such as myself. But I don't think marriage is even a remote possibility between us, do you?"

Berman spread his hands. His gold rings gleamed. He shrugged, moving his shoulders uncomfortably under his tailored silk shirt. "Why the hell not?" He stood up and paced up and down. He frowned. "Is it because of your guy George, is that it? You hung up on that wimp?"

"George has his failings," said Moira, "but I certainly don't wish to do anything that would cause him to leave me, that's true."

Berman paced up and down some more. "Goddamn it, Moira. You care about that little jerk? I'm telling ya, the kind of offer I'm making, it don't come around every day. I mean, I'm offering you a hell of a lot, you got to understand that. And I'm not just talking about money and business and like that."

"Then, what are you talking about, Hermie?" Moira asked, wondering why it was men always had to be such a chore to deal with.

"I'll tell you," said Berman. "There's things I can show you—I mean, like erotic things—that you ain't ever had done to you by nobody else. I guarantee it."

Moira raised her eyebrows. "Really?" She tried to sound bored, but secretly she was interested now. As someone who had spent a lot of his life in the pornography industry, it really was possible—just about conceivable—that Herman Berman knew some clever little perversion that had escaped her attention.

"Forget about George," he told Moira, and grabbed one of her hands between his own pudgy paws. "George is just the schmuck you like to have around, doing your chores. George—"

He broke off suddenly as the door of Moira's room opened.

And there was George, walking into the room, with Brad right behind him.

Moira and Berman looked at Brad and George. Brad and George looked at Moira and Berman. There was a long moment of silence. Berman, of course, was now respectably dressed—except that he had forgotten to put on his shoes and socks. Moira, on the other hand, was still in her laced-up black-leather dominatrix outfit.

"Oh," George said stupidly.

"Dear George," Moira said with a forced smile, "I was just telling Herman, here, how indispensable you are to me." She hesitated. and her smile faded. "Although, I distinctly told you not to come back here until the afternoon, didn't I?"

George looked back at her sullenly, and didn't reply. He glanced at Brad.

"We found a store that sold riding crops of the kind you wanted," Brad said. "But they didn't take credit cards, and we didn't have enough cash, so we had to come back."

Moira sighed and gave him a vexed look. "Very well, I'll give you some money. Although, I can't help thinking this was simply an excuse for George, here, to come and invade my privacy." Moira went over and opened her purse.

"By the way, Moira," said Brad, "I just looked for Abigail, and she wasn't in our room. Do you know where she is?"

Chapter Sixteen

Lord James Barrington hustled Abigail quickly down a long, high-ceilinged corridor. Its walls were covered with enormous gold-framed oil paintings of aristocrats. The ceiling was vaulted and lavishly decorated with heraldic crests. Elderly Lords in conservative dark-blue three-piece suits stood here and there in groups of two and three, muttering to each other, shaking their balding heads, and fiddling with their hearing aids.

"Gosh . . . I mean, it's just like I imagined it!" Abigail exclaimed.

"All fake of course," Lord Barrington said vaguely. "I mean, the original House was burned down, and this is the nineteenth-century reconstruction of the earlier architecture—quite decadent, really. Excuse me a moment, my dear. I have to consult that gentleman over there."

He walked briskly over to an official standing outside a pair of large oak doors decorated with ornate carvings. The official looked like a retired war veteran. He sported a white handlebar moustache that bristled almost as fiercely as his white eyebrows. His antique uniform was embellished with a row of medals and ribbons. He stood with his legs apart and his arms folded. His chin was almost touching his chest. He glared balefully out at the world from beneath his rampant eyebrows, as if to say: None shall pass!

Lord Barrington had a word in the ear of this elderly retainer, then stepped quickly back to Abigail.

"Thomas, here, will take you to the special visitors' gallery," he said with a quick, abstracted smile. "I'm just in time for the division. The, er, vote. I'll come and collect you in fifteen minutes, no more." Another quick smile, and he hurried away through a door marked PEERS ONLY. Could be a sign on a public toilet, Abigail thought to herself irreverently.

"This way, madam," the old guard told her. He stared at her fiercely, and Abigail blushed as if he might have somehow been reading her mind.

He led her up a stone spiral staircase—like something out of a medieval castle, Abigail thought to herself in wonder—and through a wooden door that was too low even for her to walk through without stooping.

She found herself in a cramped upper gallery that ran around the edge of the debating chamber of the House. It was like a box at the theater. The chamber itself was down below.

There were just three seats in this section—and none of the seats was occupied. Abigail realized she was in a very exclusive part of the gallery; where it ran around the opposite wall of the chamber, there were more seats, and all of them were full of visitors and journalists.

Abigail sat down and leaned out over the oak rail. She looked down into the House. It's surprisingly small, she thought. Someone standing was giving a speech, droning on in a barely audible monotone. Most of the other Lords looked as if they were asleep. Several had put their feet up on an antique table that stood between the front benches.

The speechmaker finished, then sat down to a chorus of muttered cries of "Hear! Hear!" from one side of the room and "Rubbish! Shame!" from the other side.

At the end of the chamber, a man in ermine robes and wearing a funny-looking hat, banged a gavel and said something Abigail couldn't catch. Evidently it was a signal for the vote to be counted. The Lords started getting to their feet, which for some of them was quite a challenging ordeal. A House official went around to the back benches and woke up the elderly members who had nodded off.

Abigail watched as the debating chamber gradually emptied out through two doors at opposite sides. Just outside the doors, officials were keeping a tally of how many Lords filed out. That seemed to be how the vote was counted.

Abigail waited. Minutes passed.

The Lords started tottering back in again. She looked, but she couldn't see James Barrington.

Then she heard a sound from behind her and turned around, just in time to see Lord Barrington himself. He had come up to join her.

He took the seat next to hers. The space was so cramped his knees could hardly fit behind the oak partition that fenced in the gallery.

"Hope you're not too bored," he whispered into her ear.

She took his hand. "Of course not! This is such a wonderful surprise—though I can't figure out what the hell is going on down there."

"They're starting another debate," he whispered back to her. "See the fellow getting up to speak, he's on the Conservative benches. The Labour benches are the ones on the other side. Liberals and Independents are at the end. They're called crossbenchers. The fellow presiding over the whole thing is the Lord Chancellor. He sits on that large gray cushion, which is called the Woolsack."

"Huh?" said Abigail.

"It would take too long to explain." Lord Barrington put his hand on her thigh, casually, as if by accident. "Shall we stay up here and listen for just a little while?" he said.

There was almost something suggestive in his tone of voice—and yet, surely she must be imagining it. She frowned and looked quickly at his face, but his expression betrayed no hidden meaning or feeling.

"Sure, let's stay here a little while," she whispered to him, "unless you've got more voting to do."

"No, that was the only important one." He settled himself beside her. He removed his hand from her leg and put his arm around her shoulders instead. His hand circled her body and slid across the side of her breast.

This time Abigail looked at him more sharply. Still his face betrayed nothing.

"Furthermore," said the man who was speaking down in the debating chamber of the House, "I consider it an absolute disgrace that the right honorable gentleman from East Grinsted should refer to coursing as, and I quote, 'butchery of innocent woodland creatures.' As anyone who has ridden with hounds will testify, it is a sport, sir, a fine and venerable sport whose roots extend—"

"They're debating whether to outlaw fox hunting," Lord Barrington whispered to her. "They have this same basic debate about once a year. They never reach a decision, either way. But it's a British tradition."

"Oh," said Abigail. "I kind of thought they'd be talking about things that would be, you know, of national importance."

"But this certainly is of national importance," he replied with deadpan sincerity. He slid his arm a little further around her, till his hand crept past the side of her breast and over its nipple. He rubbed his fingers gently to and fro, massaging the sensitive flesh through Abigail's thin summer dress.

She squirmed in her seat. "Hey! What the hell are you doing?" she hissed at him.

"What does it feel as if I'm doing, my dear?"

"But, in the House of Lords?"

"You must admit, in a debate as dull as this, one needs

a little diversion." He reached for her with his other hand, and thrust it blatantly down between her thighs. His fingers probed up under her skirt.

Abigail gave a little jump as he touched her clitoris through her panties.

"Come on," Lord Barrington murmured softly into her ear. "Let us have a little fun. No one can see us, you know."

Abigail glanced to either side. Each end of the gallery where she was sitting with Lord Barrington was partitioned off by waist-high paneling, and they were screened from the front also. Even the people in the visitors' gallery opposite would be unable to see anything of Abigail or Lord Barrintgon below neck level, so long as he and she sat well back.

"But someone else could come up here," she objected.

"No," he contradicted her. "I had a word with Thomas. I told him that, ah, we would prefer not to be disturbed." And he nibbled on the lobe of her ear.

Abigail flinched as little tingles spread out down the side of her neck. "You're a disgrace!" she hissed at him.

"I want you," he told her. His hand went through some contortions under her skirt. She tried to keep her legs pressed together to thwart him, but he managed to get his fingers inside her panties. He found the spot and began rubbing her clitoris insistently.

Abigail knew she couldn't hold out against it for long. She tugged futilely at his wrist, then slumped back in her seat as waves of erotic sensation rippled through her.

"On a point of order," one of the Lords was objecting down in the debating chamber. "I believe, if I am not mistaken, contrary to the assertion of the right honorable gentleman from Harrow, the Act of 1659 stated that activities on privately owned lands exceeding thirty acres should be—"

Abigail closed her eyes and lost track of this awfully proper British voice as Lord Barrington's finger worked busily on her clit. She felt herself getting all hot and wet inside.

She swallowed hard, and tried not to look as if she was getting aroused. What he was doing seemed so blatant, so obvious, she imagined that anyone could guess what was happening simply by looking at her face.

"I want you," Lord Barrington murmured again. He took her hand and pressed it to his own crotch.

His cock was huge inside his baggy pinstriped pants. Abigail closed her fingers around the long, hard shape. She felt herself gettting even more turned on.

"I think you just dropped something on the floor, Abigail," he said and gave her a meaningful look.

"What?" Abigail found it hard to concentrate on what he was saying. What was he trying to tell her?

"I think you should bend down and look for whatever it was you just dropped," he said. He kept touching her clitoris with one hand, and moved his other hand to the back of her neck. He slid his fingers into her hair. He began exerting an insistent pressure, forcing Abigail to lean over toward him.

"Hey," she said. "I don't—"

"Just bend forward," he told her. And he pushed insistently at the back of her head, his fingers twined in her hair. He urged her face toward his crotch.

He removed his other hand from her clitoris and quickly unzippered his fly. He pulled his cock out. "Come along, Abigail, my dear," he murmured to her. "Don't disappoint me now."

Abigail saw his hard, heavy cock just inches in front of her face. She tried to pull back.

Lord Barrington took hold of his penis in one hand, and kept hold of Abigail by the hair at the back of her head with his other hand. Taking no notice of her attempts to resist him, he held her head down until her lips brushed across the tip of his distended organ.

Abigail sensed the tension in his body. She heard him

breathing quickly, expectantly. Her resistance weakened; she let him push her head lower, until his cock nudged between her lips.

Abigail opened her mouth, gave herself up to the moment, and let Lord Barrington's cock slide in all the way to the back of her throat.

"Yes," he murmured. He shifted his hips, moving his cock in her mouth while he kept hold of the back of her neck should she change her mind and try to withdraw from him. "Oh, yes," he groaned, while down in the debating chamber just the other side of the thin waist-high oak partition, a member from Hull was expounding on the humanitarian practice of shooting foxes rather than letting them be torn to pieces by hounds.

"A little faster, Abigail," whispered Lord Barrington.

She responded, moving more quickly. His cock was so big, it strained her jaw muscles to take it into her mouth. She massaged the underside of his penis with her tongue, she sucked on it as hard as she could, and she moved her head up and down, up and down, making wet noises.

Lord Barrington sat with a carefully controlled expression. He watched Abigail's face pressed to his crotch. He glanced from her to the debating chamber, then back at her again. A brief smile flickered at the corner of his mouth. His face twitched as he felt the tension grow in his groin. "More," he gasped. He swallowed hard and jerked his hips up as her mouth came down on him. "Yes . . . yes—oh, Abigail!"

He suddenly grabbed hold of her head and forced her to take the entire length of him. His muscles all went rigid and his cock spurted.

Abigail swallowed the hot sticky fluid that gushed into her mouth. She swallowed and swallowed until, finally, Lord Barrington subsided in his seat, breathing hard, still trying not to show any emotion on his face.

Abigail raised her head. Carefully she licked all around the end of his cock, till every trace of jism was cleaned away. Then she kissed his penis and tucked it inside his pants.

"Did you like that, Lord James Barrington?" she murmured to him.

"Indeed, indeed I did," he whispered back to her. He reached in his jacket pocket and extracted a monogrammed handkerchief.

She took it from him, mopped her mouth daintily, and returned it. She sat up, brushed her hair back from her face, and stole a guilty glance at the Lords, who were still droning on about fox hunting.

"I guess I found what I dropped on the floor," whispered Abigail, with a sly smile.

He nodded. "Indeed." He patted her thigh and winked at her.

"So, do I get my turn now?" Abigail asked, cocking her head to one side expectantly.

Lord Barrington glanced at the debating chamber below, then back at Abigail. "I doubt there's room up here for me to go down on you," he said. He indicated the very cramped space between the seats and the partition in front.

"Oh, yeah?" said Abigail. "You mean, you get me all hot, and then you get your rocks off, and now I'm still all worked up, here, and——"

"Shhh," he reminded her, nodding in the direction of the Lords below. One of them was reading a letter from the owner of a country mansion, to the effect that if fox hunting was ever outlawed, he would renounce his British citizenship.

"Oops, sorry," Abigail whispered.

Lord Barrington put his arm around her. "I would be quite able, my dear," he told her, sliding his hand between her legs, "to satisfy you—manually."

She frowned, then realized what he meant. "Hell, I don't want a finger-orgasm," she protested playfully. "What kind of deal is that?"

142

"Then, I suggest," Lord Barrington murmured to her, "perhaps we should go elsewhere? You're quite right, Abigail, we can't leave you dissatisfied, can we? Maybe we should return to your hotel room and make sure, this time, that your needs are well and truly taken care of."

Abigail grinned at him. She kissed him quickly on the cheek. "That sounds just fine," she said. "Let's go!"

Chapter Seventeen

Meanwhile Moira was shooing George and Brad out of her room. "Remember, it has to be a twenty-inch riding crop," she told George. "With a leather handle—not vinyl —and a glass-fiber rod inside it for extra strength."

"Yes, Moira," George said dully. He lingered in the doorway and flashed a last resentful glance at Herman Berman, who was sitting complacently on Moira's bed as if he owned it.

"And when you come back, George," Moira went on, "which, incidentally, will not be before one o'clock at the earliest—when you come back, I shall test out the riding crop. I shall test it very severely, on someone who flagrantly disobeyed me this morning by walking in here, without warning, when he had been told specifically not to do so. I think you know whom I mean, George."

"Yes, Moira."

"Then, we will see you later. And you, Brad." And she shut the door firmly.

"I tell ya," Berman said, "that jerk's more trouble than he's worth. You'd be better off without him."

"Shush!" Moira gave him a warning glance, then pressed her ear to the door panels. Faintly she could hear Brad and George talking outside in the hall as they walked away to the elevator.

"I don't understand, man," Brad was saying. "Why do

you let her treat you like that?" But Moira was unable to hear George's mumbled reply.

"That Brad," she said, turning away from the door. "He's so witless. I really don't know what Abigail sees in him."

"Same kind of thing as you see in George, I figure," said Berman. "He does whatever she wants. Plus he looks good."

Moira shrugged. "Perhaps. Anyway, Hermie, where were we? You were telling me something very interesting, as I recall."

"About you and me getting hitched, you mean?" He gave her a hopeful grin.

Moira stood in front of him and folded her arms under her breasts, squashing them up close together in the skimpy leather outfit. She gave Berman a withering look and tapped her foot.

"I already gave you my answer on the subject of marriage," she said. "It doesn't interest me in the slightest. What caught my attention was your claim that you could show me erotic pleasures I've never experienced before."

"Oh. Yeah." Berman scratched his head. "Well, all right. You mean, now?"

Moira shrugged. "Of course." She stared at Berman and waited.

He got up and went and put his shoes and socks on.

"So, where do you think you're going?" Moira demanded.

"Up to my room. That's where the stuff is."

"Stuff? What stuff? Hermie, I do hope you're not going to disappoint me." Moira stepped across the room and nipped one of his plump cheeks between her finger and thumb. She gave her wrist a little shake.

"Hey, Moira, trust me, okay? Five minutes. All right?" He backed away from her.

Moira put her hands on her hips. "I'm a lady who does not enjoy being kept waiting," she lectured him.

Berman nodded nervously. He stooped, tied his shoe-laces, then turned and hurried out of the room.

Moira waited. Just as she was beginning to suspect that Berman wouldn't return, he came back carrying a stack of small, plain white cardboard cartons.

He went to the bed and dumped the cartons there. "I don't normally show this shit around," he said. He was out of breath from carrying the boxes and hurrying.

"Yes, but what on earth is it?" Moira was unable to contain her impatience. "Drugs? Clothes? Herman, I thought you were going to show me some wonderful new erotic technique. Some darling little perversion that only your twisted pornographic imagination could have invented."

"No, no, you got me wrong. It's gadgets. Gadgets to do things. See, Moira, I got talents you don't even know about. Mechanical talents. Bet you never guessed, huh? I'm like an inventor. Real good imagination, you know? Some time soon I'm gonna go into production with this stuff, a separate business. But right now there's just these prototypes."

Moira reached rudely in front of him and grabbed one of the boxes. She opened it and pulled out the item she found inside. It was like a condom, with padding. A double-walled rubber sheath with a tube extending from it to a rubber squeeze-bulb.

"What the hell is it? It looks icky."

"That's for women who like big dicks," said Berman. "See, the guy puts it on over his dick, like a rubber. Then he pumps it full of air. Or the woman can pump it up till it gets to the size she wants. Then the guy fucks her."

"I see." She wrinkled her nose. "You made this yourself?"

"Sure. Well, no, actually I didn't make it. I like did the designs. I got this guy in Van Nuys to make the prototypes from my ideas."

"And you brought all these—these weird thingies—to England with you?"

147

"Sure. I didn't dare leave 'em behind. If someone found 'em, the ideas could get ripped off. None of this stuff is patented yet. You're the only person I ever showed any of this shit to, Moira. I'm trusting you not to talk about it, not to nobody. All right? You promise?"

"Hermie, you have my word of honor," she told him wearily.

She turned the penis-sheath over in her hands. "It occurs to me," she went on, "that if a man wears this, he wouldn't feel much sensation. He'd be riding on a cushion of air, so to speak."

"Yeah, well, that's true," Berman agreed. "But it's the woman's pleasure that matters, isn't it?" He gave Moira a sleazy, ingratiating grin.

She smiled back at him demurely. "Quite so, Hermie, quite so. But it also occurs to me—I mean, I've never been terribly concerned with penis size myself—but if this thing is pumped up with air—"

"Like an airplane life jacket," Berman interrupted. "In fact, I call it a cock-jacket."

"Yes. When it has air inside it, it'll be kind of squishy to the touch, won't it?"

"Ah, well, that's true. Some women might like it that way, of course. But if they don't, you can take the air-pump bulb off and put this on, instead." He opened another box and showed her another gadget.

This was a tube with a plunger. "See, you fill it full of water," said Berman. "Then, instead of pumping air into the cock-jacket, you pump water in. Makes it a much firmer layer around the guy's dick. At least I think it would. I haven't actually tried it, on account of I've been reluctant to show any of this shit to anyone."

"Mmm," said Moira dubiously. "So what're all these other boxes? This, for instance?" She opened the very largest box and pulled out a penis-shaped gadget that trailed all kinds of wires and tubes.

"That, that's what I call Superdick," said Herman Berman with obvious pride. "It's the ultimate dildo. The wires, there, attach to—to this unit." He pulled another item out of another box. "See, it's adjustable, generates just a little electric tingle. Then you can adjust the temperature of the dildo with this controller—make it red hot, if you want a real hot fuck!" He grinned at Moira. "Or it'll refrigerate it, instead, if that's what you get off on. And it has a built-in vibrator, of course, and what I call a wriggle-rod, makes it wriggle like a belly dancer. And then if you push this plunger, Superdick gets either fatter," he demonstrated, "or longer," he demonstrated again, "or both."

He turned the dildo over in his hands, inspecting it with the satisfaction of a master craftsman. "What do you think?"

"I think," Moira said with a lascivious smile and a sudden gleam in her eye, "that we should test it out right now!"

"Yeah?" Berman looked at her eagerly. "You mean it?"

"Of course I mean it. Get all those other boxes off the bed." She gestured impatiently.

Berman hurried to obey.

Moira walked around the bed, sat on one edge, and took off her boots. Then she moved onto the bed, stretched her legs out, and reclined against the headboard. She watched as Berman removed the last of the boxes, then took his clothes off.

"My dear Hermie, I've never seen you so excited."

"Yeah, well, I tell ya, I never had a chance to test it out before." He stripped himself naked, then started strapping the Superdick around his hips.

"No, no," said Moira. "You're doing it all wrong."

He stopped in confusion. "You think so? But this is how it's supposed to go."

"Silly boy, Hermie! I'm the one who wears it, not you. Come along, now, give it to me."

He looked at her in dumb confusion. "You get to wear it? Then, who gets fucked?"

There was a moment's pause.

"Who do you think, Hermie?"

"Me?" he whined. "Up the ass?"

"Well naturally, dear." Her eyes gleamed with anticipation. "You surely don't think I would let you insert that monstrosity in my tender little pussy! Heavens, you've admitted the thing has never been tested. It might do anything to me! Really, if you want to test it out, it should be tested on—I mean, in—you. Don't you agree?"

"I guess I hadn't thought about it that way," said Berman. "But—but I wanted to give you a great time, Moira. That was the idea, to give you a superfuck with Superdick."

Moira quickly took it away from him before he could argue the point any further. "Well, if it works on you, perhaps then you can try it on me," she said smoothly. "Lie down, now, there's a good boy. On your tummy." She patted the bed.

Berman hesitated.

"Lie down!" she snapped at him. "I won't tell you again!"

Berman flinched from the edge in her voice. Without a word he stretched out on the bed.

"Now," said Moira, "let's see how this works." She started plugging the various wires and tubes into the support systems. "It's lucky I gave you that enema, isn't it, Hermie? You're all clean and ready." She giggled to herself. "This is going to be such fun!"

"Put a little grease on it, Moira, all right?" Berman said nervously.

"Yes, yes. You leave that to me." Moira strapped the hi-tech dildo around her hips and positioned the various control boxes where she could reach them easily. She smeared some Vaseline on the dildo and then kneeled between Berman's legs.

"Lift your ass, Hermie!" She slapped his bottom playfully. "And pull your knees up. I don't want this to hurt, now. Well, not too much, I guess!"

Berman groaned in anticipation. He clenched his fists and bit his lip and closed his eyes.

"Now, then," said Moira. She edged forward and pushed the tip of Superdick against Berman's puckered asshole. "Open wiiiide," said Moira, with a gay laugh.

Then she thrust her hips forward, and Superdick lunged up Herman Berman's ass with a slithery squelching sound.

Berman gasped.

Moira giggled. "How does it feel, Hermie?"

He grunted and gasped again. "Guess this is my day to get screwed."

Moira worked the dildo in and out a couple of times. "It's good for you," she told him. "You really ought to know how it feels to be on the receiving end."

She reached down and twisted a dial on the temperature control box. "Now, how's that?"

For a moment there was no response. Then Berman yelped. "Jesus fucking Christ! Feels like you shoved a red-hot poker up my ass!" He started thrashing around desperately.

Moira clucked her tongue. "Make a note, Hermie, the temperature control is far too responsive." She quickly flipped the dial to the opposite end of the scale.

"Ugh!" Berman cried a moment later. "Now it feels like you got ice cubes in there!" He wriggled and tried to reach behind for her, to make her pull out of him.

"Bad boy!" she scolded, and slapped him. "You dreamed up this gadget, so don't start complaining if it doesn't work right. Now, what does this do?" She turned another dial. This time the dildo started vibrating and buzzing.

"Eck!" gasped Berman.

"And this?" said Moira. She turned a switch.

The dildo started twisting and writhing like an egg beater.

"Arg!" Berman groaned.

"And this," said Moira. She turned a dial.

151

There was a hiss of compressed air, and the dildo started swelling up at the same time it continued buzzing and writhing.

"There, I think that's large enough," said Moira, noticing Berman's eyes bugging out and his hands scrabbling over the bed-sheets.

She turned up the last of the controls. "What's this? The one that gives a little electric tingle?"

"Nnuh!" Berman yelped.

"I thought so. Well, better turn it up all the way, to get the full effect!"

"Gaaaah!" Berman yelled.

Moira smiled sweetly. She started moving her hips in a swift rhythm, plunging the ice-cold, buzzing, wriggling, inflated, electrified dildo in and out, in and out of Berman's ass.

"You're right, Hermie!" she cried in delight as Berman coughed and gasped and winced and started gnawing the pillow into which he'd pressed his face. "This really is an experience I've never had before!"

Chapter Eighteen

Abigail and Lord James Barrington crept along the quiet carpeted corridor of the Ritz. "Shhh!" Abigail warned him. "For all I know, Brad came back here already."

"I thought you said you had told him not to return until the afternoon," said Lord Barrington.

"Yeah," said Abigail, "but I don't want to take any chances."

She turned a corner in the corridor and paused outside Moira's room. "What's that noise?" she whispered to Lord Barrington.

He joined her outside the door and listened with her. There was a strange, buzzing, whining sound, creaking bedsprings, and a low-pitched male moaning. Then Moira, giggling hysterically.

"What the hell do you think she's doing to Herman in there?" said Abigail.

"To whom?"

"Herman Berman. The guy whose party I met you at. He's my producer now, paying for this trip. He and Moira—I'll tell you later." Abigail raised her fist and rapped on the door panels.

"I should not be seen in your company, my dear," Lord Barrington told her nervously, and ducked back around the corner in the corridor.

At the sound of Abigail's knock on the door, there was

the clicking of switches, and the electro-mechanical buzzing and whining noises gradually diminished and ended. Then Abigail thought she heard Herman Berman gasping—either in fulfilment, or with relief; it was hard to tell.

Footsteps padded across to the door. "Who's there?" Moira called sharply.

"Abigail."

There was a pause, then Moira unlocked the door and opened it a crack. "What do you want?" She scowled out at Abigail.

"I—just wondered if you've seen Brad," said Abigail. "Did he come back yet?"

"He and George turned up here without warning half an hour ago. I sent them away till one o'clock at the earliest. Why? Are you planning a tryst, Abigail my dear?"

"Hell, no!" Abigail laughed unconvincingly. "Why would you think that?"

Moira wrinkled her nose. "Your hair is disheveled, your dress isn't straight, and you smell of sex."

"Well!" said Abigail, unable for a moment to think of a reply. Then she happened to glance down—and glimpsed Superdick. "My god, what's that thing you're wearing?"

"Mind your own business!" Moira snapped, and slammed the door.

Abigail turned and called to Lord Barrington: "Come on! We've got an hour or so, at least."

He emerged from where he'd been hiding around the corner. He followed Abigail into her room. "What was that you just asked your sister?"

Abigail shut the door of her room. "What she was wearing. Looked like a dildo, with all kinds of wires attached. Jesus, Moira is so weird. Anyhow, let's not think about her." Abigail grabbed hold of Lord Barrington and kissed him hard on the mouth.

He broke the kiss uneasily. "You're sure we're safe here? I'm concerned, Abigail, about your reputation—and mine."

"I tell you, it's safe. Moira said so. Now, kiss me!"

Lord Barringon looked down at her. He studied her face for a moment as if savoring her looks. He cupped her face between his hands. He kissed her gently on the forehead, then on the tip of her nose, then lightly on the lips. He slide his hand down inside the front of her dress, across her soft, cool flesh, until his fingers touched her nipple. He wrapped his other arm around behind her and kissed her again, fleetingly at first, teasing her, then harder, slipping his tongue in and out between her lips.

Abigail felt a familiar warm glow begin spreading from her crotch through her body. She put her hands behind Lord Barrington's neck and interlocked her fingers. She closed her eyes and opened her mouth wide to him. She pressed the front of her body against him, and rubbed her hips slowly from side to side. She felt the shape of his cock begin getting bigger inside his pants.

"Two orgasms in the last hour," she murmured to him, breaking the kiss for a moment. She reached down and felt the outline of his cock. "And it seems like you're still ready for more." She opened his fly, reached inside, and started fondling him shamelessly.

"I think I shall always be ready for more, with you, my dear," he told her. "Although, I thought we came back here because you were demanding your turn for satisfaction. Wasn't that so?" He smiled at her indulgently.

She nuzzled his neck and nibbled his ear. "Let's make that—our turn," she whispered. Her grip tightened on his cock, and she masturbated him slowly, holding the stiffening flesh in her fist and moving her hand to and fro, to and fro.

"Let's sit on the bed," he told her, and guided her a couple of steps backward to it. They sat down facing each other, while she kept on masturbating him.

He reached under her skirt and pulled her panties down a little way, then thrust his finger into her cleft. She kissed him on the mouth some more, and went on touching his cock, while he fingered her clitoris.

When they were both feeling thoroughly hot and horny, Abigail pulled away for a moment, kicked off her shoes, then slid her panties down her legs. "Take off your pants, Lord Barrington," she told him. "Right now!"

"I think I should undress in the bathroom," he told her.

Abigail frowned. "Huh? Why?" She tugged playfully at his belt.

"Just ... in case," he said. He stood up, looking embarrassed.

"In case of what? Christ, I've seen you naked before."

"Nakedness has nothing to do with it. I'll be back in just one second, dear girl." He kissed her quickly on the forehead, then made a quick retreat into the bathroom.

Strange, Abigail thought to herself. Then she shrugged. After all, it was somehow in character for a British Lord to have eccentric habits.

Lord Barrington came back in the bedroom in a moment, stark naked. He paused, and looked at Abigail. She was lying on the bed, one hand between her legs, fondling her clitoris, her other hand playing with her own nipples. She wriggled her shoulders, making her breasts wobble. She moved her hips restlessly while she probed inside her own cunt. "Want me?" she said with a saucy, small-girl grin.

Lord Barrington's cock began to stiffen as he stood staring at her. It pulsed and straightened until, within seconds, it stood straight out from his body, straining and ready for her.

"I guess you do want me," Abigail said, noting the physical effect she was having on him.

"I can't deny it," he agreed. "My god, Abigail, this is becoming an obsession." He strode to the bed and kneeled between her legs. He took her hand away from her clitoris and substituted his own. He fingered her clit gently but insistently.

Abigail reached for his cock. It felt so hard and hot.

"I want you in me," she told him. "You got me so horny in the House of Lords." She opened her legs wide to him.

He slid one hand under her hips and pulled them up. He held his cock with his other hand and rubbed the end of it lightly up and down between her labia. The moist end of his penis massaged her clitoris tantalizingly.

"Umm," said Abigail. She closed her eyes and wriggled her hips. Then she lifted her legs, wrapped them around behind Lord Barrington, and urged him into her.

For a moment he held back, teasing her with the tip of his dick. He clenched his fingers on her buttock, holding her so that she couldn't push herself closer.

"I want it!" Abigail complained. "Stop teasing me! I want it inside me!"

"You want this?" He inserted just the first inch of his cock and held himself there without moving any further.

Abigail locked her ankles together behind him so that he was trapped. She pulled with her thigh and calf muscles. Her heels nudged behind Lord Barrington's ass, dragging him inexorably toward her.

Still he tried to resist, but she flexed her legs and he was pulled against her, and his cock slowly sank all the way into her pussy.

"Now I'm going to keep you here," she told him with wicked delight. She squeezed her legs tighter around him, and got up on her elbows. "I'm going to make you fuck me and fuck me and fuck me, Lord James Barrington."

"Is that so?" he said with a smile.

"Yeah, that's so." She reached out quickly and grabbed his shoulder. She hauled herself up till she was in a sitting position, sitting on his cock, still with her legs wrapped around him. She hugged herself to him and rubbed her tits against his chest. She kissed him hard and pushed her tongue into his mouth. The entire length of his cock was embedded in her.

Lord Barrington fell backward, and Abigail followed him down. She unwrapped her legs as he subsided onto his back, and sat on him, like a triumphant conqueror, with his cock still trapped inside her.

"Now," she said, moving eagerly on him, "now I can get what I want—as much as I want, for as long as I want!" And she started bouncing up and down on him with a look of bright-eyed delight. Her cheeks were flushed, her nipples were clenched tight and standing out hard. Her breasts bounced and her long golden hair danced around her face as she fucked herself on him busily. His rigid cock slid in and out of her. Her buttocks smacked against him. He lay flat out under her, watching her and admiring her beauty, with a look of fatherly indulgence.

Abigail braced herself with her hands against his chest, and fucked herself as hard as she could. She gasped and made little excited noises. Then she held her hips hard down upon him and rubbed from side to side, massaging her clitoris against his crotch. She scraped her fingernails down through the tightly curled hairs on Lord Barrington's chest. She groaned and whimpered, then threw her head back and came.

Her cunt clenched on him as a series of exquisite spasms took hold of her lithe, lovely body. She savored every last tingling pulse of pleasure. And then finally, she relaxed.

"That's number one," she said with a satisfied smile.

Lord Barrington raised his eyebrows. "How many are you intending to have?"

Abigail fell forward and pressed her body close to his. She kissed him lightly. "I don't know, two or three. I've been thinking, I might as well make the most of you, since I seem to have decided to have an affair with you, after all."

"I don't know how long I can keep myself from coming," he pointed out. "You are a very sexy young woman, Abigail."

"I am, huh? Tell me." She lay and looked into his eyes. "You're beautiful, and you have that dangerous mixture of childlike innocence and a woman's sensuality," he told her.

Abigail grinned. She kissed him on the cheek. Then she started moving her hips restlessly again. "I want my second one now," she told him.

Lord Barrington laughed. "Who am I to object? By all means, do as you wish with me, my dear."

Abigail sat up on him. She shook her hair out of her face and started fucking herself on him some more—but then stopped suddenly.

She had heard the noise of a key rattling in the door of the room.

"Oh, my god," she said, and put her hand to her mouth. "It can't be!"

"Let me up!" Lord Barrington told her with a sudden look of panic on his face. "Get off me!"

"Brad, is that you?" Abigail called out.

"Yeah," came a muffled reply. The key rattled some more.

Lord Barrington grunted, and threw Abigail off him. She landed on her back on the bed. He leaped across the room to the bathroom, dived through the door, and slammed it behind him.

At the same moment, Brad opened the door into the hotel room and stood there.

Abigail lay on her back on the bed, gasping for breath. She felt her vagina gently dripping juices onto the sheets. "Hi, Brad!" she called, with a wild, desperate grin.

Chapter Nineteen

Brad looked at Abigail. Abigail looked at Brad. "Well, you're back early," she said stupidly.

"I got tired of chasing all over town with George, doing his errands for Moira." Brad shut the door and sat down beside Abigail on the bed. He admired her nakedness and grinned. "What you been doing? Masturbating?"

Abigail did a double take, then gave a shrill laugh, which ended abruptly when she realized how awful it sounded. "Why, Brad . . . how'd you ever guess?"

"You look kind of turned on," he said. He eyed her with obvious lust. Then he grabbed her and kissed her hard on the mouth. "Want me to finish the job?"

Abigail felt dizzy. She couldn't cope. Maybe she should confess the truth right now, except that—no, Lord Barrington's reputation, she had to think of that.

She disentangled herself from Brad. "No—I—uh— The job's already finished, Brad. Climaxed, I mean. Just now. I mean, you weren't here, and I was feeling horny, so—" she shrugged. "Why not!"

Brad grinned. "Oh, well, what the hell. Bad timing, I guess. Incidentally, where were you an hour or so ago? I came back then, and couldn't find you."

Abigail's mind went blank. She tried to think, but her mind simply wouldn't work. "I—" she stammered. "I—

just slipped up to see Herman. Yes—to talk about the script."

"But Herman was in Moira's room," said Brad. "I saw him."

"Yeah. Of course. I mean, that's what I discovered, when I went up to find him. He wasn't there. He was down here."

Brad frowned at her. "Abby, what's wrong?"

"What do you mean what's wrong? Christ, are you going to start asking me what's wrong again?" Instinctively she grabbed the sheets and pulled them up to her chin, as if to protect herself from him.

"Well, you're acting weird, that's all I know. Why do you keep looking at the bathroom door?"

"The bathroom?" Her voice cracked. She deliberately swallowed hard and tried to un-tense herself. "Why should I keep looking at the bathroom? You're crazy! I haven't been looking at the bathroom!"

Brad stood up. He walked toward the bathroom door.

"Don't go in there!" Abigail shouted.

"Why not?"

"Because—because there's someone in there. He came to fix the telephone and asked to use the toilet."

At the same time, she thought to herself—Christ, Abigail, you're supposed to be an actress! You ought to be able to do better than this!

And she would have been able to do better, if only she had a script.

Brad scowled at her. He grabbed the handle of the bathroom door—which, in his panic, Lord Barrington had slammed without thinking to lock it. "I'm going to get to the bottom of this," said Brad.

He opened the door wide—and revealed Lord James Barrington's naked buttocks.

Lord Barrington had put on his shoes and socks and was pulling his pants up. But his aristocratic torso was still naked. He glanced over his shoulder, saw Brad, and froze.

162

"What the hell are you doing, man?" said Brad. "Taking a shower in there? What the fuck is this?"

Lord Barrington didn't stop to talk. He buckled his belt, then bundled his shirt, waistcoat, and jacket under his arm. He whirled around, ducked past Brad, and ran out and down the corridor.

Brad glared at Abigail. "That guy was no goddamned telephone repairman!"

"No—you're right!" she cried. "He—he was a burglar! He came in here and said he'd kill me if I screamed! Oh, Brad, thank god you got here in time! You saved me!" And she flung herself at him.

He fended her off. "Christ, Abigail, we gotta catch him."

"No! Let him go! I don't want any trouble!"

Brad pushed her away and strode to the connecting door to Moira's room. He threw it open without knocking. "Moira! Quick! There was some guy in here. I think—he tried to rape Abby. Some thief or something. We got to get him."

Without waiting for a reply, Brad turned and ran out after Lord Barrington.

"Shit," Abigail muttered. "Shit, fuck." She grabbed a dress and wriggled into it.

"What's the panic?" Moira stood in the doorway. She was breathing hard and her face was flushed. Strapped around her hips, the hi-tech dildo continued to vibrate and writhe wth a life of its own.

"I've got to stop Brad," said Abigail. "This could be a terrible scandal."

"Scandal?" Herman Berman called from Moira's room. "Hey, hold it. What the fuck is happening in there?"

"I've got to stop Brad!" said Abigail, and ran out.

By the time she got down to the lobby, there was no sign of Lord Barrington—but Brad was at the front desk, waving his arms and shouting. "You mean he just ran past you and you didn't stop him? Are we talking about the same guy? Blue pinstripe suit, brown hair, in his forties, tall—"

"Just calm down, sir. Please calm down," the sedate English desk clerk was telling him. "We'll notify the police, and—"

"Calm down? He was upstairs raping my girlfriend!" Brad's shrill American voice echoed through the whole length of the vast mirrored lobby, drowning out the soothing harmonies of a string quartet playing in the tearoom. People turned and stared.

"What did you say this gentleman looked like?" asked a woman who was also standing by the front desk.

Brad went through the description a second time.

"That's what I thought you said," said the woman. She was a petite creature, barely over twenty-one, wearing a skimpy low-cut dress that revealed most of her ample breasts. She had flaming red hair hanging below her shoulders in a cascade of natural waves. Freckles and a turned-up nose made her look cute as a schoolgirl, but there was a pugnacious set to her jaw and she had sharp eyes that darted to and fro, as if she were looking to pick a fight.

"Brad!" said Abigail, running up and grabbing his shoulder. "Brad, come back upstairs. Think of the publicity!"

"You're the one he tried to rape?" the red-haired young woman snapped at Abigail.

Abigail turned and stared at her. "I— Who are you?"

"I'm the Countess of Dorset. Who are you?"

"Please, ladies and gentlemen," the desk clerk was saying. "Please, let us try to sort out this matter in an orderly fashion. I have called our own hotel detective, and—"

"You're the Countess of Dorset?" Abigail's voice was an incredulous squeak. She took in the woman's Lolita-esque face—and her mini-dress, revealing most of her breasts and legs.

"My title seems to mean something to you," said the countess, while Brad watched them both in confusion.

"I— No, you just looked kind of young," Abigail improvised.

The countess stared at her with narrowed eyes. "You rotten little liar!" she shouted suddenly. She stepped forward, drew her arm back, then punched Abigail as hard as she could on the side of her jaw.

Abigail screamed, stumbled backward, and fell on the floor.

"That was no burglar in a pinstriped suit, that was Lord James Barrington!" the countess shouted. "And like hell he raped you, you—you dirty whore!"

"Ladies, please!" the desk clerk protested.

"Hold her, Brad!" Abigail cried, squirming away across the black-and-white tiled floor of the palatial lobby, while the Countess of Dorset advanced on her menacingly with her fists clenched.

"But Abigail, is this true?" Brad protested.

"Never mind if it's true! Stop her!" Abigail winced as she felt the side of her jaw.

People were running across the lobby to see what was happening. Old ladies, Arabs, businessmen, gigolos, and debutantes started crowding round.

Then Moira appeared on the scene, pushing through to the front, no longer wearing her dildo but still dressed in her black-leather dominatrix outfit. And Herman Berman was right behind her, with nothing but a towel draped around his waist.

"This woman is insane!" Abigail screamed, pointing up at the countess. "She hit me! She doesn't even know me!"

"I don't need to know you, to know what you've been up to," the red-haired one shouted back. "When I called the House and they told me James was here, I knew what he was doing. Screwing some ugly little tart like you!"

"That's—that's the actress, Abigail van Pelt, lying there on the floor, isn't it?" someone in the crowd exclaimed.

"All right, hold it right there!" said Herman Berman,

stepping in. "We can settle this in the privacy of my suite."

"Get out of my way, fatso!" snapped the countess.

"Lady," Berman waved his finger at her, "no one talks to me like that."

The countess didn't bother to answer. She stepped forward and punched Berman in the stomach.

He coughed and doubled over, then sank down onto his knees.

The onlookers gasped. Several of them grabbed the countess by the arms. She struggled and swore at them. Voices were raised. It looked like it was growing into a total mob scene.

The desk clerk and a couple of bellboys were running around the edges of the crowd, trying to disperse it. But more people were still arriving—including George, walking into the lobby carrying a long brown-paper parcel.

"George!" Abigail cried. She wormed her way free from the crowd, while everyone's attention was distracted by the countess. "George, help!"

"Let me go!" the countess was screaming from the center of the mob. "I just lost my temper, that's all. Look, I assure you, I will not hit anyone else. This is a purely personal matter!"

"We've got to get out of here," Abigail told George. "Christ, what a mess!"

"What's happening? Where's Moira?" George asked suspiciously.

"Over there, with Herman. But this isn't her fault. It isn't anything to do with her."

"Don't try to humor me," said George. "She's been working up to this all morning. I knew she wanted to create some kind of spectacle with that Berman, and I've had enough of it." He walked past Abigail and pushed into the crowd with rude determination to get to the center.

Abigail swore and went after him. "George! You don't understand!"

Someone was helping Berman to his feet. George saw the movie producer. He was stark naked; his bath towel had fallen off when he collapsed to the floor.

"I've had it with you!" George shouted. He threw himself at Berman and started pummeling his chest with his fists.

"Get the guards from the casino," Abigail heard the desk clerk tell one of the bellboys. "They'll know how to handle this."

The bellboy nodded and ran off through a side door that led to the hotel casino in the basement.

"How dare you!" Moira was screaming at George. "How dare you hit Herman!" She grabbed the brown-paper parcel, which George had dropped. She ripped the wrapping off, revealing the brand-new riding crop she had sent George out to purchase. She raised the crop and brought it down with all her strength across George's back. She beat his bottom, his back, his neck, and then his hands, as he retreated from her, holding up his arms to protect himself.

He turned and ran, and she chased him around the Ritz lobby, knocking over giant potted ferns and sending a marble statue toppling into one of the Corinthian pillars supporting the frescoed ceiling. The riding crop whistled through the air, George leaped and yelped in pain and panic, and Moira shouted obscenities at him. Her face was contorted with rage. Her breasts bounced up and entirely out of the top of her skimpy, laced-up black-leather bodysuit.

"I'm sorry I hit you, whatever your name is," said a voice.

Abigail turned and saw that the red-headed countess was right beside her, having broken free from the onlookers who were now gaping at Moira pursuing George.

Abigail took a wary step back, though the countess seemed to have got rid of her aggressions—for the time being, anyway. "It's okay," she said, nervously fingering the bruise on her jaw.

"I'm Clarissa," said the countess. She held out her hand.

"Abigail." Abigail shook the hand warily. "I've heard a bit about you—uh, Mrs. Barrington."

"Mrs. Barrington? That's what James told you? My god, the lies he spins. Look, we must go and talk somewhere. If you can stop these friends of yours—"

At that moment three huge, blue-suited bouncers appeared in the lobby, led by the bellboy who'd gone downstairs and fetched them from the casino. They took one look at the situation. One grabbed Moira, one grabbed George, and the third started herding the onlookers away.

"All right, ladies and gents! The party's over! Please excuse the interruption, it's all being taken care of."

The chief bouncer turned to the desk clerk. "Who started all this?"

"Him," said the clerk, pointing to Brad. "And her, and her, and him, and her, and him." He carefully identified the countess, Abigail, Herman Berman, Moira, and George, with self-righteousness satisfaction.

"All right, you lot," said the pug-faced muscle-bound bouncer. "I should think the manager'll want a word with you. Step this way, if you please, sir, madam." His cockney voice was heavy with sarcasm.

Chapter Twenty

"I think it's clear," said Moira, fifteen minutes later, "that all of us have to clean up our acts." She glared at Abigail, at George, at Brad, and at Clarissa, the Countess of Dorset. All were gathered in a circle in Herman Berman's penthouse suite, while he remained downstairs dealing with the management of the Ritz.

"Now," Moira went on, "I gather, Abigail, you've been having an affair with someone."

"Well, you don't have to treat me like a fifteen-year-old," Abigail snapped back. "Good god, you're my twin sister, not my school-teacher. And for that matter, how many affairs have you had lately?"

"One too many!" George put in.

"All right, all right." Moira held up her hands. "I said we've all got to clean up our acts—*including* me and George and Herman. Does that soothe your precious ego, sister dear?" She gave Abigail a smile that looked more like a sneer.

Abigail drew in her breath to make an angry response, but Brad put his hand on her shoulder and held her back. "Let her finish, Abby."

"Thank you, Brad. Now, Abby. It's not that you had an affair, it's that you tried to keep it a secret and then slipped up in a way that could cause a scandal affecting all of us."

"She's right, Abby," said Brad. He shook his head at her reprovingly. "You could've told me, you know. I wish you'd respected me enough to tell me what was going on."

"Jesus Christ!" said Abigail, and rolled her eyes. "I thought it was all over. I didn't know the guy would hear that I'd arrived at the airport, then find me here at the hotel. And he was the one who wanted to keep it quiet, not me. And how was I supposed to know his wife would come here looking for him?"

"Not 'his wife,' please," said Clarissa. "I don't know why James told you that, but it simply isn't true."

"I'll take your word for it, I guess," said Abigail. "But how did you know he was here, anyway?"

"He had left word with his secretary at the House of Lords, that in an emergency he could be telephoned at the hotel. He's such an incorrigible ladies' man, I knew what that meant. I've had my suspicions for weeks, except I couldn't prove anything. But now," she smiled with satisfaction, "I have succeeded."

"The main thing, though," Moira put in, "is for us to be sure your fling with Lord what's-his-name is over, Abigail. Correct?"

Abigail looked uncomfortable. She thought of Lord Barrington and remembered the sex they'd been sharing when Brad had turned up and started all the trouble.

Abigail glanced uneasily at Clarissa, Countess of Dorset. The red-haired young woman was staring at her fiercely.

"All right, all right," said Abigail. "It's over. It's over! Is that what you wanted to hear?"

"Thank you, Abigail," said Moira.

"But what about you?" said Abigail. "You caused just as much of a scene yourself, down there in the lobby. You in your leather outfit and Herman in his bath towel—"

"We only went down there in such an embarrassing condition because you claimed someone had raped you and run out of your room, dear," said Moira.

170

"Oh, yeah?" said Abigail. "Then, why did you go chasing George around the lobby with a riding crop?"

"Well," said Moira, "I must admit, George and I have a few things to settle. George, sweetie, you just heard Abigail promise to be good in the future. Can we have your promise, too?"

"If you lay off Herman!" George shot back.

"George dear, I think you've forgotten what I told you, about the importance to me of business relationships," Moira said smoothly.

"Bullshit!"

Moira made a tut-tutting noise. "George, if you don't do as I say—" She broke off as the door into the penthouse suite opened and Herman Berman walked in, now wearing a robe over his bath towel. He stopped and looked around the circle of faces. He noticed Clarissa and glared at her. "I'm gonna sue you for assault!" he shouted.

"Mr. Berman, I'm terribly sorry," she told him. She stood up and walked over to him. She walked with a well practiced wiggle, shaking her tits and her ass simultaneously. She stopped very close up to Berman and laid one of her dainty hands on his shoulder. "I was so emotional, I didn't know what I was doing."

"Yeah?" Berman grunted. "The fact remains, lady, you punched me in the gut."

"I know, it was awful of me. Is there any way I can make it up to you?" She batted her eyelashes.

Abigail watched from across the room, and felt a savage twist of jealousy. This was the countess Lord Barrington had talked about. The woman he had said wasn't interested in sex, and was quite happy for his lordship to screw around with other women. Abigail clenched her fists in silent rage.

"Well," growled Berman, unaware of the torments Abigail was going through. "I suppose, lady, we can settle out of court. A couple grand will fix it."

"Oh dear," said Clarissa. "I'm afraid that's not possible." She looked melodramatically sad about it. "I suppose I'll have to face a lawsuit, after all, since I cannot pay you. And the publicity will be so damaging." She gave him a meaningful look.

Berman went quiet for a minute. Obviously he was suddenly contemplating newspaper headlines, describing how a 100-pound woman knocked him down with one punch while he was wearing nothing but a bath towel in the lobby of the Ritz.

"Well, we'll talk about it later," he muttered. "We'll work something out."

"The main thing I want to know, Herman," said Moira, "is what happened downstairs between you and the hotel management."

"They don't want this in the newspapers any more than we do," said Berman. "I gave 'em a little cash, to cover the damage, and so far as they're concerned, nothing ever happened. No one was here and nothing happened. But there's one condition: we got to move out right now."

There was a general murmur of dismay from all concerned.

Berman shrugged. "What the hell. We'll go to the Savoy. That's an okay hotel. I already called 'em and made reservations. So get your bags packed and we'll go get a cab."

"I really think we still have a few things left to sort out," said Countess Clarissa, when all the luggage had been taken down and loaded into a capacious London taxi.

"You still worried about what I said up in my room, about the lawsuit?" said Berman. He looked less sure of himself now, out in the alien surroundings of a British city. He grimaced. "Forget it, kid. I was just mad, that's all. You keep quiet about it, and so will we."

"Oh, I understand." She fluttered her eyelashes at him again, and gave a little wriggle that made her big breasts wobble from side to side under the thin fabric of her skimpy dress.

Berman found himself staring. He blinked and deliberately looked back up at her face. "Then, what's the problem?"

"Oh, no problem, Mr. Berman. I just think we should talk things over a bit more. About what to do if news of all this gets about. Someone recognized Abigail, you know, during all the—the goings-on. And—well, what am I supposed to say, if a newspaper reporter starts asking me difficult questions?" She stared at Berman with wide-eyed innocence.

The little bitch was angling for some cash to keep quiet, Abigail realized. First she'd hit Berman in the stomach, now she was hitting him for a bribe. Incredible.

"All right, all right," said Berman, sensing which way the conversation was going. "You want to come with us to the Savoy? We can talk there. But we got to get moving. We got a tight schedule. Abby's on a talk show tonight, so we got to get our shit together."

Clarissa shook her head. "I'm afraid I can't come with you now," she said. "I have a—a pressing engagement. But I could meet you later this evening. For dinner, perhaps?"

Berman sighed. He was getting impatient. "For dinner. Sure."

"There's a simply lovely restaurant called Du Rollo, in Soho," said Clarissa. "Can we meet there? At eight-thirty? I really think it would be worth your while, Mr. Berman." She treated him to some more eyelash-fluttering and breast-bouncing.

Berman reached in his pocket for his diary. "Spell the name of the place," he said, and wrote it down. Then he got in the cab, where George and Moira and Brad were already waiting.

Clarissa turned to Abigail, still standing out on the Piccadilly pavement. She seized Abigail's hand. "I do hope

173

you've forgiven me," she gushed, gazing directly into Abigail's eyes. "For hitting you, I mean. I was so upset. I get so mad when James is naughty behind my back."

"Yeah, well, enough said," Abigail replied. She tried to pull her hand away, but Clarissa kept hold of it.

"I just don't understand why he has to be unfaithful to me, do you?" Clarissa persisted. She looked at Abigail's body with frank, appraising eyes. "I mean, what have you got that I haven't got?" And she looked down at herself, as if admiring the size of her own tits.

Abigail glared at her. She searched for some kind of come back. "Maybe I give good head," she blurted out. "Even in the House of Lords visitors' gallery," she went on savagely.

"Oh!" Clarissa cried, in mock dismay. She put her hand over her mouth. "Really!"

"You ever think of going into acting?" said Abigail. "You got real talent." With that, she climbed into the taxi and slammed the door before Clarissa could begin to think of anything else to say.

It took fifteen minutes to drive to the Savoy, unload the cab, get the room keys, have the bags taken up, and call room service for lunch.

Abigail ate some indifferent cheese sandwiches in her new room with Brad, and reflected that it was true what people said about British food.

"I'm real pleased it's all over," Brad said to her, methodically unpacking his bags for the second time that day, and stashing his clothes neatly in a bureau. "I knew something was going on, Abigail. I wish you hadn't tried to pretend it was nothing. But there's no hard feelings, I want you to understand that. Hell—I mean, the guy was a British aristocrat. How can I compete with a fellow like that?" He smiled at her uneasily. There was uncertainty and unhappiness in his expression.

Abigail squeezed his shoulder. "You're a nice guy,

Brad," she told him. To herself, she thought: And we all know what position nice guys finish in.

"Well, I think you and me have something special," Brad went on while he laid out his socks with single-minded precision: black ones to the left, then the brown ones, then the mixed colors. "We can make a great team, Abigail. I mean, the future's wide open for us."

"Sure, Brad," she said vaguely. She went and stared out of the window and wondered where Lord Barrington had run off to, and whether she'd ever see him again, and what the story really was with so-called Countess Clarissa, who wasn't James Barrington's wife and probably wasn't a countess, either. More likely a striptease artist. Abigail wished she had Lord Barrington right there in front of her—to interrogate him. . . .

Meanwhile in Moira's room, she and George were finishing the little discussion they had begun back in Berman's suite at the Ritz.

"I'm warning you, George," Moira was lecturing him, in the cutting, strident voice he knew so well, "my dealings with Herman are business dealings, and that includes all forms of sex and role-playing. And if you interfere again, I'll see that you suffer. And I mean really suffer!"

"But it's not right," George whined. "How do you think I feel, seeing you and him together? It's an insult. It's degrading. I can't stand it. And I won't! I won't stand for it!"

Moira stared at him steadily. "George, I have warned you." Her voice was suddenly much quieter—and somehow more deadly, as a result.

George shifted uneasily, but he wouldn't back down. "If you go on having sex with Berman, and not with me," he said, looking at her deviously, "you know, I can make things pretty difficult."

Moira stood up slowly and walked over to him. She was dressed in normal clothes now—a simple, tan business

175

suit and low-heeled shoes. But she still walked with the same swagger as if she were wearing her dominatrix outfit.

She stopped and put her hands on her hips. She glared at George, where he sat on the side of the bed. "Are you actually daring to threaten me, George?"

He swallowed hard. "Just remember, I know everything that happened at the hotel today," he said. "I saw it all. I know all your secrets."

"You little worm." Moira turned and strode to the phone. She grabbed it and gave a savage tug. The wire came out of the wall.

She threw the phone down on the floor, stamped her foot on it, and pulled the other end of the wire out of the phone itself.

"What are you doing?" said George. He stood up quickly and backed off a couple of steps, looking nervous.

Moira didn't answer. She strode toward him.

George suddenly realized he had crossed some invisible line, from what was permitted to what was never tolerated under any circumstance. He panicked, and tried to make a break past Moira to the door.

She casually tripped him, and he fell sprawling on the floor.

She sat down on him, twisted one of his arms up behind his back, and then his other arm as well. Quickly, angrily, she tied his wrists together with the phone wire.

"No!" George gasped. "I didn't mean it. I'll be good!" His voice quavered with a mixture of fear and excitement —because, after all, her anger always turned him on. To be the center of her attention, that was all he asked.

Moira grunted with the effort of tugging at the wire, making the knots tight. "Bend your knees," she snapped at George.

He squirmed on the floor. "I'm sorry, Moira, I—"

She grabbed his hair and jerked his head back, making him wince. "Bend your knees!"

Dumbly, still lying on his stomach on the carpet, George obeyed.

Moira seized his feet and flipped them under the wire binding his wrists behind his back. She rolled the wire around over the toes of George's shoes so that his legs were caught and he was hog-tied.

"Oh please, Moira!" he begged her. "You're not going to leave me here like this?"

Moira went into the bathroom and came back with a washcloth. Then she opened one of her cases and took out some panty hose.

"You will open your mouth, George." And she kneeled down beside him and jerked his head back by the hair again.

Too scared to defy her any more, George opened his mouth.

Moira stuffed the washcloth in, then wound her panty hose quickly across George's face to hold the cloth in place. She knotted the panty hose securely behind his head, then stood up.

"That's what happens to little worms who threaten to talk too much," she smirked. "You will stay like that, George, until tomorrow morning." She gave him a sharp jab with the toe of her shoe. He made smothered noises behind his gag. "You will probably not get much sleep in that position. Your legs will suffer horrible cramps, and your back will begin to ache excruciatingly. That is your punishment for threatening me. Tomorrow, I will decide whether to let you remain as my secretary."

She crouched down beside him. She had vented her anger. He looked quite adorable, now, all trussed up and helpless. "George," she said, ruffling his hair with something vaguely akin to affection, "you're such an idiot."

Then she went and finished unpacking her clothes.

Chapter Twenty-one

The BBC sent a limousine to take Abigail and her party out to the Shepherd's Bush studios, where the talk-show appearance was to take place. She relaxed in the soft leather upholstery with Moira and Herman and Brad as the big car drifted through London traffic in the gloved hands of its impassive, implacable chauffeur.

"So where's George?" Abigail asked Moira.

"Oh, he decided not to come," Moira answered with a barely perceptible hesitation.

"I do hope you and he got everything straightened out," Abigail said, smiling at her sister with total insincerity.

Moira flashed Abigail an irritated look. "Completely," she said.

"He 'cleaned up his act'—the way you wanted all of us to?" Abigail persisted. "No more nasty little scenes? I do hope we don't have to leave this hotel too."

"All right, you two," Berman interrupted. "Knock it off." He glared at Abigail, then at Moira.

"Sorry, Hermie dear." Moira patted him on the cheek. "You know Abigail likes to rub me the wrong way sometimes."

"I said knock it off!" Berman repeated. "Later, all right? All right. Now, Abby, you got the talk-show topics memorized?"

"Of course, Herman."

"The host's name—"

"—is Michael Larkin. Herman, I *have* done this kind of thing before. I *am* a professional actress."

Herman sighed. "Just checking."

Abigail realized she had been using the same acid tone of voice on him as she had on Moira. And Herman didn't deserve it.

Abigail bit her lip. She stared out of the tinted-glass window at the lights of London as the car moved through evening twilight. She was still on edge, she realized; still obsessed with Lord Barrington; still secretly wanting to see him, despite her promise not to and despite his lies to her about his alleged wife.

Abigail turned back to Herman. "I'm sorry I snapped at you," she told him, modulating her voice. Then she turned to Brad, sitting beside her, and squeezed his hand, more out of guilt than anything else. She gave him a quick smile.

He stared back at her uncertainly.

"Let's try to have things settle down the way they were back in Los Angeles a few days ago," she said, trying to make the words sound right. Maybe if she said it, she'd end up believing it.

"That's what I've wanted all along," said Brad.

Abigail shrugged, and tried to look carefree. "Then, we've got nothing to worry about, have we!"

"I still got something to worry about," Berman muttered.

"No, Hermie," said Moira. "You haven't. I promise you George will never again—"

"I'm not talking about that jerk," said Berman. "I'm talking about the redhead. Countess what's-her-name." He shifted uncomfortably in his seat. "Wish I hadn't told her I'd meet her later."

"Then, don't go," said Moira.

"And risk having her blab about what happened?" Berman shook his head. "No, she's got to be fixed. Paid off—or whatever it is she wants."

"Then, we'll all come with you," said Moira. "All of us. Right?" She looked at Abigail and Brad.

"Sure," said Brad. "I think it's important, right now, that we all stick together."

"Abigail?" Moira asked.

"Oh, absolutely," Abigail agreed, coming back to reality with a jolt. She had been dreaming, again, of Lord Barrington, and wondering if she dared go looking for him at the House of Lords. . . .

The talk-show host had a respectable, BBC-approved British accent, but he'd obviously learned all his routines from American television.

"And so you're stepping into another actress's shoes in this film *Some Sweet Summer,* Abigail," Michael Larkin said, studying her as if she were the most fascinating person ever to have appeared on his program. "That must be an awkward situation."

"Oh, not really," Abigail said with a bright smile. From the corner of her eye she saw which camera she was on, and adjusted her position fractionally, to present her best profile. She checked herself on the color monitor screen above the stage, over the audience. "Each new role has its own challenges, Michael," she went on blandly. "I just have to learn this one faster than usual."

"Have you ever met Helen Hingley?"

"Never. But I've seen several of her pictures. I think she gave a truly fine performance in *Tender Nights.*" To herself, Abigail thought: It stunk. That movie was a piece of shit. But, diplomacy—always diplomacy. She wanted Herman to be proud of her.

". . . true Helen's hard to work with?" Larkin was asking, as if the question had suddenly occurred to him.

"There are all kinds of rumors in this business," Abigail answered smoothly, giving the response she had prepared to this inevitable question—the response Larkin obviously guessed she would have prepared. "I really try not to listen to the gossip. I know most of it simply isn't true.

As regards *Some Sweet Summer*," she spoke the title of the movie with careful precision, to make sure everyone heard it clearly, "I'm lucky to have a wonderful producer, Herman Berman. And I'll be working with a good friend of mine from California, Brad Milford. I think he has truly exceptional talent."

"Really?" Larkin nodded with politely faked interest. "But I don't think I've heard his name."

"Well, he's in the audience right now, I think," said Abigail. "Brad?"

Obediently the director turned a spotlight and one of the cameras onto the studio audience. Brad stood up. There was polite applause.

There, Brad, Abigail thought to herself. She'd given him what he had wanted. So, now she could feel less guilty about the way she'd gone behind his back with Lord Barrington. Part of the debt was paid, at least.

". . . pleasure to have you with us, Abigail," Larkin was saying, winding it up, "and I hope you thoroughly enjoy your stay in England."

"Thanks, Michael," she said, putting her head on one side and treating him to a warm, glowing smile.

More applause. Then one of the cameras dollied in for a close-up of Larkin's face. "With us next week, the Prime Minister of Quango-Quango, and Stephanie Stephens, the best-selling author of *How to Make a Man Do Anything You Want*." He paused, and wiggled his eyebrows suggestively. Then back to his homely, friendly grin. "Join us then."

The theme music cut in. The red light on top of the camera went out. On the monitor screen, Abigail saw they were rolling the credits. She stood up, shook hands briefly with Michael Larkin, and walked offstage.

Herman was waiting for her. "Great, just great, Abby." He looked relieved. "Christ, I was beginning to think this whole trip had some kinda jinx on it. But you did great. Guess we ain't gonna have no more problems from now on, right?"

"Right," Abigail told him, trying to match his tone of breezy confidence, though secretly she still felt uneasy, somehow—as if the problems were by no means over.

"Want to introduce you to some friends of mine," Berman went on. "In the British movie business, came down here tonight specially to see you." He took her arm. "Bloodsuckers and asslickers, every last one of them," he muttered into her ear. "But we got to go through the motions."

Then there were the introductions, a couple of faces she knew vaguely from other work she'd done in England, a lot of compliments, meaningless small talk. A BBC hostess, looking stiff and strained and awfully formal, came around with a tray of small, weak drinks.

"Anyway, we got to get going," said Berman, when Brad and Moira arrived backstage. "Got an appointment—"

"But Mr. Berman," complained a fat, perspiring man holding a notebook, "could I get just a few words with Abigail? I'm Charlie French, of the *Express*. You know, I do the show-business gossip column, and I've got a couple of inches to fill in tomorrow's edition. We could include a picture, and—"

Berman wavered. He turned to Abigail. "You want to do it?"

She shrugged. "Sure." She wanted to prove to him she really could be agreeable, professional, and reliable.

Berman glanced at his watch. "I got to go, though, Abby. You join us at the restaurant? We're late already."

"That's fine," said Abigail, talking without thinking. "I'll take a cab."

And so Berman and Moira and Brad left, to go to their rendezvous with Countess Clarissa, and Abigail stayed and talked to the journalist for twenty minutes, telling him the usual harmless, witless trivia that he could regurgitate in his column. She was relieved he didn't ask anything about the Ritz; evidently news of that incident hadn't gotten around.

183

Finally Abigail freed herself and walked out of the main doors of the studios.

The night was cool and damp. She shivered, wishing she'd brought a wrap or a jacket with her. She was used to LA, where the weather never changed suddenly like this.

Abigail grimaced. The studios were located at the edge of London; it was crazy of her to think she could just hop in a cab. She realized she would have to go back in and find one of the staff, and get him to call a taxi for her.

But at that moment a uniformed chauffeur walked up to her out of the darkness. "Miss van Pelt?" he inquired, looking at her uncertainly.

Abigail stopped. "Yes?"

The chauffeur shuffled his feet, as if he were embarrassed about something. "Your car is waiting."

"A car for me?" She frowned. "Well, thanks. But— Who arranged this? Mr. Berman?"

"Yes, madam. Compliments of the BBC. This way, madam." He led her away from the studios, down a short concrete sidewalk to a black Austin Princess waiting in the darkness with its lights off and its motor idling.

"There you are, madam," said the chauffeur, opening the rear door with a flourish.

"Well, thanks," Abigail said again, and stooped to climb into the car's dark interior.

Hands reached for her. Two hands. One grabbed her wrist. The other grabbed her neck. Someone had been hiding in the shadows in the back of the car, someone waiting for her.

Abigail gave a little cry and tried to pull back.

But the hands hauled her in. And the chauffeur slammed the door behind her.

Chapter Twenty-two

"Let go of me!" Abigail screamed. "Help! Somebody help!"

"Quiet, be quiet!" the man in the car shook her angrily. And suddenly she recognized the voice.

"Barrington! What the fuck is this?"

Meanwhile the chauffeur had got into the front of the limousine, which was separated from the passenger space by a glass partition. He started the motor. The car drew smoothly away down the dark London street.

"What do you think you're doing?" Abigail dug her fingernails into Lord James Barrington's wrists and finally shook his hands off her. "Let me out of this goddamn car."

"Abigail, Abigail, please, my dear," he said, trying to soothe her. "Calm down, I didn't mean to—"

"Then, why'd you do this to me? Why'd you freak me out like this?" She could see his face, now, intermittently lit by street lights as the limousine cruised along. He was looking at her as if her reaction surprised him.

"I was merely trying to be discreet," he explained, and reached for her again.

She knocked his hand away. "Discreet. That's a nice word for it."

"But you don't understand!" There was a tormented tone in his voice. Suddenly he lunged toward her in the dark interior of the car. He grabbed her head by the hair and pressed his mouth onto hers.

Abigail kicked and struggled. "No!" she gasped.

"I have to have you," he told her. "I couldn't stay away. Nothing else matters. Nothing." He tried to kiss her again. His breath was warm on her face. His strong body was tense, and his hands felt hot against her skin.

She fought him, but he dragged her down on her back on the rear seat, ignoring her protests. She pushed out at him with her hands, but he knocked her arms aside. He fell on top of her. Her breasts were a soft cushion under his chest. He forced his mouth on hers while she tried to turn her face away. Her body writhed underneath him. He jammed his knees between her legs and pushed his crotch against her.

Abigail gasped and cried. She pummeled him with her fists.

Lord Barrington grabbed her wrists and forced them down above her head. He held both her wrists in one hand and kept her pinned under him with the weight of his body. He paused a moment, getting his breath back, and then started undoing the buttons down the front of the dress she was wearing.

"Damn you!" Abigail gasped. She craned her neck; lying under him, on the rear seat, she had an upside-down glimpse of streetlights and shop signs moving past the car windows as it continued smoothly down the London street. She saw the back of the chauffeur's head as he drove the car, paying no attention to the scuffling in the back.

"Damn you, Barrington. Let go of me!"

"I can't," he told her. "I want you too much." He thrust his hand inside her dress and grabbed her breast. He kneaded the soft flesh and pinched the nipple, and groaned softly. Then he slid his hand around her body and down behind her ass. He clenched his fingers on her buttock, so hard that it hurt. With angry passion he jerked her hips up against him and ground against her.

She felt his cock pressing against her through the fabric of his pants.

Abigail closed her eyes and swore silently to herself. She couldn't stop him, with words or force. He was going to have her. And wasn't that, in a way, what she'd been fantasizing about?

She didn't resist as he roughly pulled her dress up and starting fingering her cunt. His hands were clumsy, and they shook with his intense desire for her. He pushed two fingers inside her.

The car went around a corner, and Lord Barrington's weight shifted. Suddenly he lost his balance. Feeling himself falling, he clutched Abigail to him.

Together they landed on the carpeted floor in the back of the limousine. Half-heartedly Abigail started struggling again. But he grabbed her shoulders and forced her onto her back, then fell on top of her once more. He opened his fly and his cock jumped out, big and hard and hot. He pushed it clumsily between Abigail's thighs.

"I want you," he gasped again, rubbing his clothed body over her nakedness. He touched her face, mauled her breast, ran his fingers down her flesh, then took hold of his cock. He forced her legs open and put himself into her.

Abigail cried out, half in pain and half in surrender. Instinctively she drew up her knees so he could enter her more easily, without it hurting.

He started fucking her like a man obsessed. His body moved violently up and down, like a marionette pulled by strings. The sound of his breathing was loud in her ear. His hands were all over her, feeling her, savoring her flesh.

It was impossible for Abigail not to respond. However much he'd lied to her, she still lusted for him. He'd forced himself on her now—but only because he couldn't contain his desire for her. That itself was a turn-on—he made her feel totally irresistible.

She wrapped her arms and legs around him. He

jerked against her, his cock stabbing in and out, his hips grinding from side to side.

Abigail bit her lip and felt the sensations build.

Suddenly she groped for Lord Barrington's face, seized it between her hands, reared up and clamped her lips onto his. She pushed her tongue into his mouth. She raised her hips off the floor of the limousine and bumped her crotch against his. She twisted and gasped and stiffened, and then she came.

As her cries of fulfillment died away and she relaxed under him, Lord Barrington redoubled his efforts. He moved in a frenzy, fucking her in a flurry of thrusts. He lay with most of his weight on her, her breasts flattened under his chest. His hips moved in spasms.

She buried her face in his neck, smelled his cologne, felt his racing heartbeats, and heard his frantic gasps for breath. His movements became erratic as he reached the limits of his strength. He twitched and made a high-pitched whimpering noise. Then all his muscles went rigid, and he clutched at her. He started coming in her.

His climax seemed to last for a long time. He flinched and whimpered with every little spasm.

Then, after it was over, he just lay on top of her on the floor of the limousine, while it cruised on through the London streets.

Lord Barrington's cock gradually shrank and finally pulled out of Abigail's pussy. His breathing slowed. He swallowed hard, reached in his pocket for a handkerchief, and mopped his brow.

"Give that to me," said Abigail. She took the handkerchief from him and mopped herself between her thighs.

Then she folded the white linen and handed it back to him.

He took it from her. "I'll keep this, as a memento," he said with a strange look in his eyes.

"How romantic. How wonderfully romantic." She wriggled out from under him and got up onto the seat. She started trying to untangle her hair. Deliberately she turned away from Lord Barrington and looked out of the window.

"Abigail?" He laid his hand tentatively on her leg.

She didn't answer.

"I'm sorry I scared you," he said. "It was pure thoughtlessness. I was simply afraid of being recognized if your friends saw me. And—I'm sorry for forcing myself on you. But I just had to have you." He fumbled with his clothes, trying to straighten them.

"Do I ever have a say in it?" she said, keeping her voice level.

Lord Barrington sighed. "You're right, of course. I should have been more—more restrained. But after this afternoon, I was so aroused by you, I couldn't contain myself."

"I met your wife," Abigail said casually. She finished fiddling with her hair and started buttoning her dress.

"What?" Lord Barrington stopped and stared at her. Then he reached for a switch and turned on the interior light in the back of the limousine. "What did you say?"

Abigail blinked in the sudden yellow radiance. She saw that the limo had been fitted out with no expense spared. A bar, a built-in TV, lots of walnut inlays and silver trim, very plush.

She glanced at Lord Barrington. His hair was sticking up, and his tie was crooked. He was staring at her, as if he were afraid of her.

For the first time, Abigail felt she had some control over the situation. "You look a wreck," she said, still keeping her voice level and offhand.

Lord Barrington peered in a vanity mirror set in one corner of the limousine's passenger compartment. He ran shaky fingers through his hair. "But what did you say about my wife?"

"Met her in the Ritz, after you ran out. She was there looking for you. Seems your secretary at the House of Lords let something slip."

His expression of shock turned to one of panic. "Are you serious? Oh my god."

189

"Interesting woman, Clarissa," said Abigail, really beginning to enjoy herself now. "Of course, she told me she's not your wife at all." Abigail smoothed her dress down, sat back and folded her arms. "So I guess you lied to me," she said, deliberately hardening her voice.

"I—I really can explain everything," Lord Barrington said.

Abigail laughed without much humor. "I certainly think you'd better try."

"But what did Clarissa say?"

Abigail paused, then shook her head. "I'm not going to tell you another damned thing," she said flatly, "till I get the truth out of you."

Chapter Twenty-three

"Mr. Berman! I'm so sorry I'm late."

Countess Clarissa wriggled her way between the tables of the restaurant and stopped right beside Herman Berman.

He turned to look at her and found her big breasts on a level with his face, and only a couple of inches away.

He blinked and flinched back in his chair. She was wearing a new outfit: a bright red dress with a deep V-neck that exposed even more than the dress she'd been wearing previously—if that were possible. Its skirt was longer, but had a slit up the side almost to her hips.

"Afraid you weren't going to make it," Berman said meaninglessly.

"Oh, I couldn't possibly stay away," she gushed. "You're all such interesting people, and I'm sure you have so much to tell me." She smiled and managed to look erotic and predatory at the same time.

"I, uh, suppose you already met my friends," said Berman. "Miss Moira van Pelt, the Hollywood agent. And Brad Milford, he's got a part in the new movie I'm producing."

"I never really got introduced properly before," said Clarissa. She focused intently on Brad. "You're an actor! How exciting! Can I come and sit beside you, Mr. Milford—uh, Brad? I've never sat next to a real Hollywood actor before. Such a handsome one, too!" She giggled and wiggled her way to an empty chair beside Brad. She slid into it, folded her arms under her breasts, and leaned forward on the table till her shoulder was touching his and her tits were very nearly falling out in front of him. "I think it was you I met in the lobby of the Ritz this morning," she went on. "When you were talking to the man at the desk and I was looking for—"

"Seems to me we agreed to forget that little incident altogether," Berman cut in. He drummed his fat fingers on the tablecloth.

"Oh, of course!" Clarissa put her hand to her mouth. "But that's why I thought I should meet you, Mr. Berman, so I could get it quite clear in my head what did happen and what didn't, and what you want me to say or not say. I do hope you can, um, do something for me—to help me keep it all straight in my silly head." She stared at him with big eyes.

Berman's face twitched. He stopped drumming his fingers and, unconsciously, clenched his fist. "Now see here," he began, "if you're trying to threaten—"

"Herman," Moira interrupted. She flashed him a warning look. Then she turned to Clarissa with one of her icy, professional smiles. "Let's not discuss business until we've eaten our meal," she said. "We've only had the appetizer so far; why don't you join us for the main course? We'd be delighted for you to be our guest. And perhaps you'd like something to drink?"

"Yes, I'd like a tequila sunrise," said Clarissa, making herself comfortable. "Thank you. But where is your sister?"

"Still at the studios," Berman said shortly. "She'll be joining us."

A waiter stopped at the table, gave Clarissa a menu, and took her drink order.

"It must be awfully exciting, being an actor," Clarissa said, staring at Brad again as if she could barely concentrate on the menu with him sitting beside her.

Brad looked down at her bulging tits, then seemed to realize he was staring and deliberately looked at the table in front of him. "Well, I guess there is some truth to that," he said. "I guess acting is kind of exciting, when you get down to it. Certainly the prospects are just incredible."

Moira looked at Berman and rolled her eyes. Berman's face remained grim.

"Do you have lots of female fans?" Clarissa was going on. "I bet they're all over you!"

Brad's face turned slightly pink. Her come-on was ridiculously blatant, but that didn't stop it from being effective. "Oh, hell, I haven't had that many parts in movies yet," he said with self-conscious modesty.

"Oh, you!" giggled Clarissa, and gave him a playful nudge.

"Your drink, madam," a waiter interrupted, placing the glass in front of Clarissa.

"I wonder," Moira cut in from the other side of the table, "could I taste that? I'd like to see how they do a sunrise over here."

"Of course," said Clarissa, handing the glass across.

Moira held it by the rim, so that her hand concealed the drink from Clarissa. She unbent her little finger, which had been holding a small tinfoil packet of white powder. The powder emptied neatly into the drink. Moira swilled the liquid around and she pretended to take a sip.

"Tastes bitter," she commented, discreetly dumping the tinfoil on the floor as she passed the glass back with her other hand.

Clarissa took it and sampled the drink. "Does a bit, doesn't it?" She shrugged and took a much larger swig. "But as I was saying— Brad, do tell me more about yourself. And your work. Is it easy working with— What was her name again? Abigail? I should think after a while the two of you would get on each other's nerves." And she watched Brad with her big, soulful eyes.

* * *

"Clarissa is not my wife," said Lord Barrington. He sighed. "Not yet, anyway. God knows, she's trying to arrange it."

"Oh?" Abigail sat with her hands clasped in her lap and watched him calmly.

"She's a very difficult woman, Abigail," he said, looking at her as if he hoped she might sympathize with him.

"My heart bleeds for you, James," she said in a deliberately matter-of-fact tone. "But how can a woman like Clarissa imagine, in her wildest dreams, she could ever marry you? Is it simply because she's a countess?"

Lord Barrington sighed. "Well, she's not, actually. That was just our little piece of make-believe. You see, she's always had a yearning for status, Abigail, which is why she has this fantasy about marriage. So I tried to make her feel better by inventing a title for her. It's meaningless, you know—the 'Countess of Dorset.' Dorset doesn't even exist any more. That county was eliminated when they revised the boundaries. I deliberately made up a blatantly silly title for her so that, if anyone challenged it, we could just laugh and say it was obviously meant as a joke."

"Ha ha," said Abigail.

Lord Barrington gave her a sick smile. He still seemed to be hoping she'd take pity on him.

But Abigail was by no means through with him. "So how did Clarissa get hold of this idea of marriage in the first place? I don't suppose, James, you encouraged her little fantasy at all?"

There was an uncomfortable silence. "Well, not much," he said.

"Jesus Christ." Abigail sighed and looked out of the window at the streets of London, still moving past as the limousine cruised slowly along, taking her she-didn't-know-where.

She turned back to Lord Barrington. "You really proposed to that little piece of trash, didn't you? The truth, now." She glared at him warningly.

"Well I did say something about marriage," Lord Barrington admitted. "When I was a bit drunk one night. And she did take it seriously. But you must believe me, Abigail, when I say that you mean much more to me than Clarissa does or ever did. I want to get rid of her, Abigail. I just don't know how to shake her off."

"What's stopping you?"

Lord Barrington sighed and spread his hands. "I was, ah, indiscreet in the past, and she knows some things that, really, it would have been best for her not to know. Frankly, I'm hoping to avoid scandal."

Abigail frowned. "I don't get it. She's blackmailing you into continuing to have an affair with her?"

"Ah, well, it's the affair and—and the money. I have been supporting her, and she has rather expensive tastes." He rubbed his hand wearily across his forehead. "God, Abigail, it's such a mess." He looked at her beseechingly.

"All because you couldn't resist it when she pushed her tits in your face," Abigail said.

"Well, I suppose that did have something to do with it."

"Yes, I suppose it did," she agreed, mimicking his serious-sounding British accent. "My god, when I think of what you originally told me—your wife the countess, who isn't interested in sex. What a sob story! I can see why you made up that one instead of telling me the truth: that she's a little nymphomaniac who must've fucked your brains out."

"I wish you didn't have to be so blunt, Abigail."

Abigail nodded. "Sure. I bet you'd prefer it if I beat around the bush and didn't call it the way it is. That'd make it much easier for you, wouldn't it? Isn't that what you British like to do?"

She sighed. She realized she had vented the last of her anger. "All right," she said, in a softer tone, "I'm sorry I yelled. But what the hell are you going to do? Try to buy her off? She'll bankrupt you. She's obviously got a nose for money. She's trying to get Herman to pay her to keep quiet about an embarrassing little scene at the Ritz, after you ran out. I'm sure she'll hit you next, now she knows you were there with me."

"No doubt," Lord Barrington agreed. "I've been trying to humor her, Abigail. Hoping in due course she would get tired of me and find someone new."

"You mean you've been screwing her and buying her clothes and stuff, to keep her from complaining too much, but at the same time you've been introducing her to all your friends."

Lord Barrington winced. He nodded without speaking.

"You're in the shit, Barrington," Abigail said, and realized that, despite herself, she was beginning to feel sorry for him after all. "Still, I guess that's your problem. Lord knows I wouldn't know how to begin to help you sort it out. I got troubles of my own." She glanced at her watch. "I'm supposed to be helping Herman talk turkey with your friend Clarissa right now, as it happens. Where the hell has your man, here, been driving us, anyway?"

"Toward the West End." Lord Barrington's tone was still totally gloomy. He gave Abigail another beseeching look. He reached out and put his hand on her knee. "Abigail, can you ever forgive me? You mean so much to me, you know."

"I do, huh? I don't know, Barrington. Ask me next week. Oh, shit, I forgive you. What does it matter?"

"Thank you, my dear. It matters to me." He stared at her some more.

Abigail felt uncomfortable. She glanced out of the window again. "So is this West End near the part called Soho? That's where the restaurant is where I'm going."

"Soho is in the West End," said Lord Barrington. "But Abigail, can't you—can't we— I was hoping we might even spend tonight together?"

She shook her head firmly. "No way. Listen, you know I've been hung up on you, but frankly, you've been nothing but bad news for me. And I think I was crazy to get hooked in the first place."

"But Abigail!" he moaned. "Surely, if my life settles down, we could——"

"Maybe when you've shaken off Clarissa, and when I've shot my scenes with Brad and am not tangled up with him any more—maybe then. Maybe."

"Oh." He stared sadly at her.

"Come on." Abigail leaned across and kissed him quickly on the cheek. "Don't give me the lost-and-lonely treatment. I can't take it. Damn it, if you're so desperate for my company, Barrington, you can watch me on TV. The talk show I taped just now will be aired tonight at ten. Watch it on your set," she nodded at the little color television built into the limo, "while you're driving home."

"No," he said. "I never watch television. I can't stand it."

"Suit yourself," Abigail said. And then something connected in her head.

"Wait a minute," she went on. "You said, today, you discovered I was in Britain when you saw me arriving at the airport, on TV. You said you always watched the morning news show. Didn't you? Jesus, were you lying to me then as well?"

"Oh. That," said Lord Barrington. "Well, just a little white lie, Abigail."

"But why, for god's sake? And if you didn't find out from the TV news, how did you know I was in London?"

Lord Barrington shrugged. "I suppose there's no harm in telling you now. Your sister's secretary, George, telephoned me at the House of Lords this morning and told me you were in London. He said you were dying to see me, but too proud to admit it. He asked me not to let you know he'd told me, because you might be angry with him for interfering."

Abigail sat and played the whole story through her head.

She remembered when she had been drunk and drugged on the plane and confessed to George all about Lord

James Barrington. She remembered a strange devious look that had come over George's face.

Then she remembered how Brad had gone out with George, that morning, but had come back to the hotel early, and had caught her with Barrington.

"That little fink," she muttered. She clenched her fists. She turned to Lord Barrington. "Look, you want to patch things up between us?"

He nodded. "Of course."

"Then help me out right now. Take me to the Savoy. Moira said she left George there. You can help me find what that devious little bastard has been up to."

Chapter Twenty-four

Clarissa was giggling uncontrollably. "So then," she said, swaying to one side and falling against Brad, "so then I left home and ran off with this traveling salesman. He didn't have much money, but I got him to nick all the cash out of his company till. We went to the Grand Hotel in Brighton for two weeks, till we'd spent it all, and then I turned him in to the cops and told 'em he'd—he'd taken advantage of me!" She lost her balance and stuck her elbow in the roast duck she'd been eating. She giggled again, uncontrollably. "Can you believe that? It was so funny! They put him inside for six months!"

"Fascinating," said Moira, with a meaning glance toward Herman Berman. "You have so many stories, Clarissa. And they're all so entertaining."

Clarissa's giggles subsided. "I s'pose I shouldn't be saying all this," she said, and frowned as if she couldn't remember where she was or what she ought to be doing. "I feel so peculiar. My god, I should have had something to eat before I had that tequila." She raised her elbow and peered at the greasy duck sauce on it. "Here, Brad—" she nudged him "—lick my elbow."

Brad had had several drinks, trying to keep up with her. He seemed totally dazzled by her. "Lick your elbow?" he said with a silly grin. "You're crazy!"

"No, no, I mean it." She stuck it toward his face. "Tell

you what, if *you* suck my elbow, *I'll*—I'll—" She started giggling again, making her breasts wobble.

Brad leaned forward and obediently licked the sauce off her elbow. She ruffled his hair and kissed him on the cheek. "I knew you'd do it for me!" she said with witless delight.

"Herman and I have to have a word about something," Moira said. "If you'll excuse us for just a moment?"

"Oh, go ahead. Don't worry about me!" Clarissa waved her other arm airily while Brad continued licking her elbow. "Oooh, Brad, you've got such a rough tongue, it tickles! Oooh!"

Moira stood up and took Berman's hand. She guided him to the end of the restaurant, near the rest rooms. "I think we've got enough, don't you? She said it in front of three witnesses, assuming Brad can remember any of this tomorrow, which he will if we remind him. If she ever threatens us, we have enough to put her in prison." She folded her arms and gazed at Berman with cheerful satisfaction.

"Yeah. Yeah, absolutely. I could see the way you were working, Moira. Very smart. What the hell did you slip her?"

"Methedrine crystals and a Quaalude, ground up and mixed together. A little goes a long way. I keep it to sniff it, but when I saw her order that drink, with all the salt around the edge of the glass I figured she'd never notice the taste."

"Right. Right. Well, let's get out of here."

"Herman." She placed the palm of her hand against his chest. "You will remember that I did this little favor for you."

He grinned. "If I know you, you ain't ever going to let me forget."

Meanwhile, at the dinner table, Brad had licked Clarissa's elbow clean. "There, Clarissa. Did I do a good job?" He gave her a silly drunken grin.

"Wonderful, you're wonderful," she told him. "So now

you get your reward. Oh! Silly me." She picked up her napkin and threw it down it between her chair and his. "I've dropped my napkin on the floor. I better pick it up!"

She pushed her chair back, and clumsily got down on the floor on her knees. She ducked under the table, fumbled between Brad's legs, and undid his zipper.

"What's going on?" Moira demanded, returning with Berman to the table. "Where is she?"

Brad twitched in his chair. "Uh, she dropped her napkin." He reached under the table, and there were scuffling noises.

The restaurant was not crowded, but people a couple of tables away heard the sounds and turned to stare.

"What the hell?" Moira bent down and peered under the table. The tablecloth was large; it hung down on all sides, concealing Clarissa. But it didn't take much imagination for Moira to guess what was going on.

Clarissa had reached into Brad's fly—she easily overcame his feeble resistance—pulled his cock out and started sucking it greedily.

She wrapped both arms around behind his hips, so there was no way he could pull back from her. She moved her head quickly and expertly and sucked on him as hard as she could. Within moments his cock was completely erect.

Brad gasped. He looked quickly to either side and saw people watching him, although no one but Moira and Berman had figured out, yet, exactly what was happening. Brad's face turned bright red. He tried to hold Clarissa's head between his hands, under the table, to stop her. But he was clumsy—and part of him didn't *want* to stop her anyway. The sensations coming from his crotch were incredible.

She sucked the entire length of his cock into his mouth, held it there, then let it pull slowly out while she wiggled her tongue from side to side and massaged him under the tip of his penis, where it was most sensitive. Then she swallowed him again, and repeated the process.

"Get her out from under there!" Moira hissed.

Brad gulped. He grabbed hold of the edge of the table. "I can't!"

Moira's face twitched. She turned to Berman. "Sit down," she muttered at him.

"Huh?"

"Sit down! What else can we do? Try and drag her out? Everyone would realize, then. We're trying to cover up scandals, not create new ones. My god, I'll kill the little bitch for this! Sit down, Herman, and pretend nothing's happening. I mean it!"

"Yeah. Sure." He did as she said.

The two of them sat and faced Brad.

Brad's mouth was open, and he was breathing hard. From under the table came distinct sucking noises.

"So, uh, what sights do you want to see tomorrow?" said Berman, in his loudest American accent.

"The Tower of London," Moira said grimly, and equally loudly, to conceal the noises. "Where they locked people up and beheaded them." She stressed the word "head."

Brad groaned. He put his elbows on the table, leaned forward, and clutched his face in his hands. "Jesus!" he muttered.

Clarissa was nodding her head, moving it to and fro as fast as she could. Brad's big fat flesh went in and out, in and out of her mouth. He squirmed in his chair and made involuntary hip movements. All his muscles were knotting up.

"After that," said Moira, through clenched teeth, "We can visit Madam Tussaud's. The Chamber of Horrors shows what they used to do to people for crimes against law and order."

"I'd like to see that," said Berman, sounding quite sincere. He imagined the exciting tortures and whippings that would be depicted. Then, realizing he had drifted into fantasy-land, he guiltily brought himself back to the present.

The sucking noises were increasing to an almost inhuman tempo. Brad gulped. His eyes bugged out. He slapped both hands on the table. His fingers curled, grabbing at the tablecloth and digging in. A wineglass fell over with a crash.

"Will there be anything else, sir, madam?" said a waiter, pausing on his way past.

"I think we better get the check," said Moira. "Our friend, here," she glared at Brad, "seems not to be feeling well."

"Gaaah!" Brad cried. His hips jerked. His chair tipped. He fell against the table. His cock started spurting into Clarissa's mouth. She clamped her lips around him and swallowed the salty jism, drinking every drop.

"Right away, madam," the waiter said. He glanced curiously at Brad, then shrugged and walked to the other end of the restaurant to add up the bill.

Brad slumped back in his chair. He slowed his breathing. "I'm sorry!" he gasped. "I couldn't stop her! I tried, Moira, I tried! But she just kept on—" A dreamy look came into his eyes.

"Yes, Brad," said Moira.

Beside her, Berman was watching Brad with a mixture of anger and envy.

Clarissa emerged from under the table. She stood up unsteadily. Her face was flushed and her hair was mussed. "Here it is!" she cried, holding up her napkin. "Silly me! I don't know why it took me so long to find it!" And she daintily dabbed jism from the corners of her mouth.

"There you are, sir, madam," said the waiter, bringing the check. "Forty-two pounds and thirteen pence, including VAT." He gave a little bow. "I hope you enjoyed your meal."

"Pay it," Moira snapped at Berman. "I'll get her out of here." She stood up and grabbed Clarissa's arm. "Come on. Time to go."

"Not without Brad!" she cried. "I couldn't leave without him!"

"I'm coming," said Brad, quickly getting to his feet.

"You just did!" said Clarissa, and giggled inanely.

"Zip your fly," Moira hissed at Brad, and then hustled Clarissa out of the place.

Chapter Twenty-five

Meanwhile Abigail was leading Lord Barrington into the Savoy.

"I still don't quite understand," he said, "what you have against this fellow, George."

"You will." Abigail stopped at the front desk. "The key to my room, please?" she said to the clerk. "I'm Moira van Pelt."

The clerk frowned at her for a moment, remembering Moira as having short dark hair rather than long blond hair. But since Abigail was identical to Moira in every other respect, the clerk had to conclude his memory about hair color must be incorrect. So he went and got the key and gave it to Abigail without a murmur.

A couple of minutes later Abigail opened the door of Moira's room and walked quickly in, with Lord Barrington right behind her.

She stopped when she saw George trussed up on the floor. "Oh, my god!" she said. "So this is what Moira meant when she said she'd had a talk with George and he'd decided to stay at the hotel. Help me untie him, James."

Lord Barrington carefully shut the door of the room and then peered down at George. "For heaven's sake, Abigail, does your sister engage in this kind of activity very often?"

"Yeah." Abigail picked at the knots in the phone wire holding George's wrists behind his back. George, still lying on his stomach where Moira had left him, craned his neck around to see what she was doing. His eyes looked plaintive, and he made muffled noises behind his gag.

"George and Moira have a little game they play," Abigail said as she loosened the wire. "She likes being dominant; he gets off on submitting to her. Except that, sometimes, the game gets out of hand." And she freed George's wrists completely and threw the phone wire aside.

George slowly moved his shoulders and arms and rolled onto his side. Inch by inch he straightened his legs from the position where they had been bent up behind him. He winced.

Abigail grabbed the panty hose that had been wrapped around his face and mouth, and pulled it off. George spat out the washcloth. He gasped and groaned.

"Cramps?" said Abigail.

He nodded. "She warned me it would give me cramps." He winced again. "But it was my fault, Abigail. I threatened her. I was terrible to her. I can't blame her for what she did to me." He slowly managed to sit up on the floor, and started massaging his wrists.

"Your sister sounds like a monster," Lord Barrington said to Abigail.

"That's the way I've always seen her," Abigail agreed. She turned back to George. "All right, now listen, George. We didn't come back here just to play the Good Samaritan with you. I'm pissed as hell and I want some straight answers. And—and if I don't get them, maybe we'll tie you up again or something. You certainly don't look in very good shape to defend yourself, right now."

George managed to straighten one of his legs completely. He flinched from the cramps and the pins and needles in his skin. "I don't understand, Abigail. Why are you mad at me?"

Abigail drew a deep breath. "All right. Moira sent you

out shopping this morning, didn't she? So while you were out, you went to a pay phone and called Lord James Barrington, here, at the House of Lords."

"You are Lord Barrington?" said George, eyeing James with surprise.

"Hey, just answer the question, all right?" Abigail told him.

George paused. "Well, yes, I did telephone—"

"We know you did. James admitted it to me. So you told him to go visit me at the Ritz, right? And then you fixed it so that Brad would turn up at the hotel and catch me and James in bed together. Isn't that right?"

"Oh no!" George exclaimed. "No, of course not! Abigail, maybe I shouldn't have interfered, but I just wanted you to be happy. You were so miserable on the plane, but you said you weren't going to contact Mr. Barrington—I mean, Lord Barrington—so I thought I would try to help." He stared at her with wide, sincere eyes. "Why would I want Brad to discover you with this man, anyway?" he went on. "I wouldn't want to make life unpleasant for you, Abigail."

She laughed sourly. "No, but I think you decided that if you caused trouble between me and Brad, it would screw up the movie deal, and that, in turn, would split up Herman and Moira. You just wanted to cause as much trouble as possible, to spoil things for Herman and Moira, so you could get Moira back for yourself."

"It's not true!" George complained.

Abigail glared at George, where he sat on the floor, massaging his cramped limbs. "All right, James, let's tie him up again."

"No!" George wailed. "No, please! Honestly, Abigail, I wanted the best for you!"

Meanwhile, outside in the street, a taxi had drawn up in front of the Savoy.

"Where are we?" said Clarissa, as she stumbled out of

the cab. She leaned against it with one hand and held her head with the other. "My god, everything's going round and round."

Moira got out of the cab, and then Berman. "Have you got cash?" Moira snapped at Brad as he climbed out.

"Uh, yeah." He fumbled in his pockets. "But I don't understand this British money too well, Moira."

"Too bad. It'll be good practice for you. Pay the driver, then join us upstairs. Come on, you." She grabbed Clarissa's arm.

"I don't understand," Clarissa mumbled petulantly. "Where are we? I want Brad."

"You've had enough of Brad, kid," said Berman, grabbing her other arm and hustling her into the hotel, past the disapproving gaze of the uniformed doorman.

"But why've you brought me with you?" Clarissa complained as they strong-armed her across the lobby.

"Can I have my key, please?" Moira said to the man behind the desk, ignoring Clarissa. "I'm Moira van Pelt."

The clerk stared at her. Once again he tried to explain to himself how Moira could be alternatingly blond and brunette. A wig?

He turned and checked the keys. "I already gave you your key, Miss van Pelt," he said with a bemused look.

Moira thought for a second. "I see," she said. She turned to Berman. "Come on. Abigail must be here. What the hell is that sister of mine up to now?"

"But I don't understand!" Clarissa wailed as Moira and Berman frog-marched her into an elevator.

The elevator doors slid shut. "We brought you back with us because right now your head is too fucked up to make sense of what we want to tell you," said Moira.

"Huh?" said Clarissa.

Moira tapped her foot in impatience. "My dear, you met us tonight to blackmail some money out of Mr. Berman, here."

"Uh. Oh. Well, not exactly, I mean—"

"Yes, you did. Well, your attempt has backfired. Right

now you're too drugged to understand, but when the effects wear off, you'll realize you have told us altogether too much for your own good. You have already incriminated yourself, my dear, so your cheap little blackmail attempt is liable to backfire against you, if you ever pursue the matter."

The elevator doors opened, and Moira dragged Clarissa out. Clarissa was frowning as if it hurt her head to think. "What do you mean, 'when the effects wear off'?" she asked. "Effects of what?"

And then she stopped still. She tried to pull her arm out of Moira's grip. "You drugged me!" she shouted.

"Oh, Christ," groaned Berman. "Not another goddamn scene. Get her into your room, Moira. Quick."

"You put something in my drink!" Clarissa shouted. "You fucking bitch, I'll rip your hair out!" And she vented a shrill scream and threw herself at Moira.

Berman watched, horrified—but, at the same time, with guilty fascination—as Clarissa grabbed Moira by the hair. Moira hadn't prepared herself for the attack, and she lost her balance. She fell backward and went down under Clarissa.

Clarissa kept hold of Moira's hair and started banging her head against the floor. "You and your fancy talk," she was shouting. "You're scum! Scum and filth!" She banged Moira's head on the floor again, then grabbed the neck of Moira's dress and ripped it open to the waist.

"Herman!" Moira cried. "Herman! Help!"

Berman circled around the two women. He hesitated.

"Keep your distance, fatso," Clarissa snarled, drugged and crazed but meaning every word. "Else I won't punch you in your fat stomach, this time—I'll punch you in the face!"

Berman gulped. Fierce women always frightened him; that's why they turned him on so much. Faced with a dominant female, his legs always turned to jelly. He stood and stared at Clarissa, and didn't move.

"Herman!" Moira screamed again. "Herman, goddam-it, why don't you help me!"

"I— I'll go get help," he muttered. "Maybe Brad—"

"You stay put," Clarissa shouted at him. "Or else!"

"Oh," said Berman. He swallowed hard again. Just watching Clarissa was starting to give him an erection.

"Damn you, Herman!" Moira screamed. She tried to rear up under Clarissa to free herself.

Clarissa grabbed Moira by the neck and slammed her back down against the floor. Then she ripped Moira's dress some more, grabbed her bra and pulled it off in one savage movement, and sank her fingernails into Moira's breasts.

Moira screamed in pain and rage. She brought her knee up into Clarissa's crotch, and threw the girl off her.

Clarissa fell onto her back and grunted as she hit the floor. Moira went after her. She started punching Clarissa with her small fists. She punched Clarissa's stomach, her breasts, and her shoulders. But she didn't know how to hit. The blows were childish and ineffectual.

Clarissa lashed out quickly and grabbed Moira's wrists. She held them and tried to get up off her back, while Moira tried to force her down again. Both women grunted and gasped with the test of strength. Moira's naked breasts quivered as she flexed her muscles. Bright red lines showed across her pale flesh, where Clarissa's nails had raked her.

Clarissa took a deep breath and heaved up with her right arm. The surge of strength overcame Moira's resistance. Clarissa threw Moira off her.

Moira landed on her stomach. Clarissa scrambled up and fell on Moira's back. Once again she seized Moira by the hair—and, this time, banged Moira's face repeatedly into the carpet.

"Herrrrmaaaaan!" Moira wailed. "Heeeelp!"

But Berman had already decided, once and for all, not to get involved. "It's your own damn fault!" he shouted defensively. "You fixed her drink. You wouldn't do it my way. Always so damned sure of yourself. You better take what's coming to you." Surreptitiously he slipped his hand in his pocket and started playing with his cock while he watched the two women writhing on the floor. He began breathing heavily. "It's been nothing but trouble, this whole trip," he shouted at Moira. "You talked me into this deal, and look where it's gotten us."

"I'll kill you for this, Herman!" Moira screamed.

"Shut up!" cried Clarissa. She banged Moira's face into the carpet again, then grabbed the neck of her dress and pulled it as hard as she could. The garment had already been ripped open at the front. There was a terrible tearing sound as Clarissa pulled the dress right off, in long strips of torn cloth. She tossed it aside, leaving Moira wearing nothing but high heels and panties.

Moira moaned and squirmed around so she was no longer on her face on the floor. She reached for Clarissa. Her fingers curled like claws.

Clarissa drove her fist into Moira's stomach. Then she dug the fingernails of both hands into Moira's shoulders and dragged them down, across Moira's breasts, across her belly, to her panties. Clarissa ripped the panties off, then continued her fingernail treatment down Moira's thighs.

Moira covered her face with her hands and screamed. "Stop it!" she cried. "Stop it! It hurts!"

"Huh! You can dish it out, but you can't take it!" Berman said with a crazed grin. His cock strained inside his pants. He gasped. He fingered himself, getting close to orgasm.

Clarissa sat on Moira's hips. All the fight had gone out of Moira. Bright red lines, where Clarissa had gouged her flesh, extended all the way from her shoulders to her knees. "Leave me alone!" Moira moaned.

"Teach you to fuck me about," Clarissa was saying. She grabbed one of Moira's breasts and twisted it savagely. She slapped Moira's face as hard as she could—first one cheek, then the other. Then she reached down and started tugging Moira's pubic hair.

"Yes!" Berman gasped. "Yes!" And suddenly he came inside his pants. He fell back against the wall, his eyes bugging out as he stared at Clarissa punishing Moira. A wet stain appeared at his crotch.

"Brad!" Moira cried. "Where's Brad? Oh, goddamn you all! George! George, where's George?"

She drew in a deep breath. "George!" she screamed.

Chapter Twenty-six

"What on earth is happening out there?" exclaimed Lord Barrington, hearing distant shouts echoing along the hotel corridor.

"I'm more concerned with what's happening in here," said Abigail, still glaring at George and trying to figure out whether he could really be telling her the truth.

And then Moira's final scream echoed down the hall and filtered through the door into the hotel room: "Geeeooorge!"

"That's Moira!" George exclaimed. "She sounds as if something terrible's happening!"

"Now, just hold on a minute," said Abigail.

"But she needs me." George scrambled up onto his feet.

"She needs you?" said Lord Barrington, with a frown. "Was that how she expressed her need for you earlier, by tying you up and gagging you and leaving you here for hours?"

"Yes, yes, of course," said George, as if the question were moronic.

"Moira can wait," said Abigail, catching George's arm. "Whatever it is, she can wait till we've finished our business, here."

"No! No, she needs me! I can tell!" He twisted out of her grasp, ran and opened the door, and disappeared down the hall.

"I can see we're going to get thrown out of *this* hotel, too," said Abigail. She sighed. "Come on, James, let's go see what the fuss is all about."

"My dear—" He hesitated. "Perhaps we should be more circumspect, and stay here. Or, even better, go to your room until all this has, ah, blown over?"

Abigail put her hands on her hips. She stared at him. "You're a coward," she said with sudden conviction. "Respectability, status, all that stuff—it's all bullshit, to cover up the fact you're chicken."

"Abigail, really—be reasonable!"

She looked at him with distaste, then turned her back and went to the door while Lord Barrington stood nervously and watched her go.

Meanwhile George ran down the hall and came upon the fracas. He took one look. "Moira!" he cried. "What's she doing to you?"

"Better stay out of it, son," said Berman, leaning against the wall and clutching his crotch. He licked his lips guiltily while he continued to ogle the fighting females.

"George! Help!" Moira cried.

George stepped forward. He grabbed Clarissa by the neck of her dress and hauled her off Moira. "How dare you!" he cried. "How dare you hurt Moira!"

"George," Moira moaned. "Oh George, you're wonderful. Thank you! Thank you!"

"Let go of my dress, fuckface," Clarissa swore at George. But she was out of breath. She'd expended most of her energy on Moira. And she still couldn't keep her balance too well, when she was standing up.

George carefully kept himself behind Clarissa and seized her neck in the crook of his arm. He held her like that, not quite sure of what to do next. "Are you all right, Moira?"

"Yes. I mean, no." Moira got up slowly from the floor.

At that moment, a little way back along the hall, there was the sound of elevator doors opening.

Everyone froze, realizing suddenly how the scene

214

looked: Berman gasping and stinking of come, Moira stark naked with her clothes and underwear lying in shreds on the carpet, Clarissa struggling in George's grip with her dress all rumpled.

Brad stepped out of the elevator. He stopped and stared. "What's this?" he said, surveying the scene with total disbelief.

At the same time, Abigail came running down the hall from Moira's room. "Are you people crazy?" she cried.

Moira was the first to collect her wits. "All right, we better get back to my room," she snapped. "Quickly! We can settle this there." She grabbed a piece of her dress and held it across her nakedness.

"Oh no," said Berman. "Count me out of this. I've had it up to here with you. You people are a buncha screwballs." He folded his arms and scowled at everyone.

"Herman, what are you talking about?" Moira wailed.

"I'll see you later," he said. "Maybe." He turned and started toward the elevators.

"Oh Hermie," Moira called after him, summoning the last of her strength. "Hermie dear. Your crotch is dripping."

"I still don't understand," Brad was saying.

"Neither do I," said Abigail. "Moira, where are your clothes? What is this?"

Moira turned and glanced at Clarissa. who was still held helpless in George's grip. "This is all your fault!"

"You drugged me," Clarissa croaked, her throat constricted in George's grip.

"Moira! Is that true?" Brad exclaimed.

"Moira's right," Abigail cut in. "We can sort this all out in her room." She hustled everyone back along the corridor.

They reached Moira's room and went in. Lord Barrington was still there, sitting nervously on the edge of one of the beds. He stood up in surprise as Abigail was followed into the room by Moira, unmistakably naked. Then his look of surprise turned to pure panic as George

215

arrived, still holding Clarissa. "Oh no!" Lord Barrington wailed.

Clarissa saw Lord Barrington. A surge of anger gave her sudden new strength. "You! You bastard!" she shouted. She flailed her arms and writhed and freed herself from George's grip. She went running across the room, knocking everyone out of her way. Lord Barrington retreated with a cry of dismay.

But he had nowhere to hide. Clarissa butted him with her head. The blow sent him stumbling backward till he hit the wall.

Clarissa paused for a second and took a deep breath. "This is for everything," she shouted. She swung her leg and kicked him as hard as she could—in the balls.

"All right," said Abigail. "Someone's got to take charge here, and it might as well be me, since Moira's in no condition to do so, and Herman's gone to his room." She stood with her hands on her hips. She eyed the others, who had circled around her in Moira's hotel room.

Moira herself was stretched out on one of the beds, moaning and whimpering melodramatically while George clucked his tongue and tenderly applied antiseptic to the scratches Clarissa had inflicted.

Clarissa was sitting as far away as she could, close to Brad, who had his arm around her protectively. Clarissa was glaring at Lord Barrington, who cowered abjectly beside Abigail, clutched his wounded crotch, and groaned softly from time to time.

"All right," said Abigail. "Let's get this straight. Clarissa, you grabbed Moira and beat her up because she drugged your drink? Is that right?"

"I can't deny it," Clarissa admitted, adopting her wide-eyed innocent look. "I'm sorry, I don't know what came over me. I have this terrible temper, and under the influence of—of whatever it was they gave me, I quite lost control."

216

"Bitch!" gasped Moira, and George patted her soothingly.

"Is she seriously hurt?" Abigail asked George.

"Just scratched," said George, with a resentful look at Clarissa. "Badly scratched," he added.

"Seems to me you got what you deserved, Moira," Abigail said with secret satisfaction.

"How dare you!" Moira cried feebly, getting up on her elbows. "She assaulted me!"

Abigail shrugged. "If you slip someone a drug, I think that's a risk you should take. Now, George—you still claim you weren't trying to cause trouble for me, when you called James?"

"I swear it, Abigail. I wanted only the best for you."

"All right, I'll believe you. What the hell, I'm losing interest in his lordship, as each hour passes."

"But Abigail," Lord Barrington moaned.

"Now, Clarissa," Abigail interrupted, "you were going to try to blackmail Herman, weren't you?"

"Blackmail!" Clarissa exclaimed, still with the wide-eyed innocence. "Oh, no!"

"Cut the crap!" Abigail shouted. "We know what you were up to. So let's put it this way: do you promise to stay the hell away from Herman, and from Moira, after this, if they don't bother you?"

Clarissa fidgeted. "All right, I promise," she said in a more subdued tone, flashing Abigail a mean look.

"Now, Brad," said Abigail, "what's happening with you and your new—uh, friend, here?"

"Well, you cheated on me, Abigail," Brad said defensively. He hugged Clarissa more tightly to him.

"But earlier today you were telling me you forgave me for it. So what's happened now?"

"She sucked him off under the restaurant table," said Moira, getting up feebly onto her elbows. "That's what happened."

Brad turned bright red.

"I did no such thing!" Clarissa exclaimed from beside him.

"The color of his face says that you did," Abigail said with a smile. "I must say, you know how to find your way through to a man's heart. You like Brad, huh?"

"Well, he is rather irresistible," said Clarissa. "But my dear Abigail, I mean, I never meant to steal your man away from you."

"Like hell. This is your way of getting back at me for what happened between me and James, here. But that's cool. If you and Brad have hit it off, that's fine. I've just about had it with his lordship. I'll tell you, I'm planning to take a raincheck from relationships in general for a couple of months, and work on the movie. To hell with men." She paused uncertainly. "If there still is a movie. Anyway, have we settled everything? Moira, are you happy to let things lie now?"

Moira gave Abigail a reproachful look, then sniffed and turned her face away.

"Good," said Abigail, realizing this amounted to her saying yes.

"But I'm certainly not content with this state of affairs," said Lord Barrington. "Abigail, how can you talk about me so callously? And Clarissa—" He looked uncertainly from one woman to the other. "Do you intend to run off with this—this actor?"

"We can sort this out down in my room," Abigail interrupted. "You and me, James, and Clarissa and Brad. Now that we have things straight with Moira and George, we can leave them here in peace."

Chapter Twenty-seven

"You're sure you don't resent what's happened between me—me and Clarissa?" Brad asked Abigail anxiously as they walked along the corridor to Abigail's room, with Clarissa and Lord Barrington following behind, ignoring each other in icy silence. "I mean, it's kind of sudden," Brad went on. "And I'm not entirely sure how it happened. But there is this kind of magnetism between us—"

"Between her mouth and your crotch?" said Abigail. She unlocked the door of her room.

"You don't have to be crude about it," he said with a hurt look.

Abigail ushered everyone in. "Brad, you and I had a good time in LA. But I've come to the conclusion it won't work, to have an affair with someone at the same time I'm making a movie with him. All right?"

"Oh. Uh, yes, I guess." He looked confused.

"Take my word for it. In fact—" Abigail thought quickly. "In fact, I think perhaps we ought to get separate rooms, Brad. I want to talk to Lord Barrington, here, with Clarissa. He has some explaining to do—not that he hasn't done enough already, but this time I can check his story as we go. While I do that, why don't you go downstairs to the lobby, Brad, see if the hotel has an extra room, and register yourself into it? All right?"

He looked even more confused. "I guess so. I'll come

back up here, and collect my stuff, and, uh, Clarissa, after that?"

"Sure." She gave him a quick smile, then shooed him out.

She shut the door and turned around. She saw that Lord Barrington was whispering something urgently to Clarissa, over in the far corner. He looked as if he were trying to win her over.

Clarissa drew back from him and shook her head. "Forget it!" she told him loudly. "I'm not going to lie for you any more, James. If that's what you told her," Clarissa glanced at Abigail, "that's your problem."

Lord Barrington flinched. He glanced at Abigail anxiously.

"In fact," Clarissa went on, with a resurgence of her temper, "in fact, James, why don't you and I end this mess between us right now? Seems to me I'll have a lot less trouble dealing with someone like Brad."

"This is all very interesting," said Abigail, walking over to them. "Why, James, you don't look very happy. But I thought you told me you wanted to get rid of Clarissa. I thought you said you couldn't wait for her to leave you."

"Er," Lord Barrington began. "Abigail, you can't believe anything Clarissa says. This conversation is pointless. Why don't you and I—"

"His lordship is scared shitless," Clarissa cut in, "because if I kick him out, he won't be able to pay his own rent."

"What are you talking about?" said Abigail.

"I've been supporting him," Clarissa said with a shrug, as if it ought to be obvious.

"*You* supporting *him*?" Abigail stared from her to Lord Barrington in disbelief. "But he told me you wanted to marry him to get *his* fortune."

"Fortune!" Clarissa started giggling. She looked at Abigail and shook her head. "That's wonderful! Oh, he makes up such great stories! I suppose you think just because he's a lord, he must be rich, is that it?"

"Something like that," said Abigail. She glanced at Lord Barrington. He stared back at her with an expression of total misery. Without warning, he slumped down on the edge of the nearest bed and covered his face with his hands, totally unable to cope.

"Let me tell you," Clarissa said to Abigail, totally serious now, "being a lord is worth nothing. Do you realize, my dear, what he gets paid for attending a debate? Five pounds a day! Ten American dollars! He inherited his title, plus a little cash, which he immediately spent. He's been living off women ever since."

"Wait a minute," said Abigail, wondering how far to trust this dangerous redhead. "I've been getting the distinct impression that it's you who exploits people and live off them—if you'll excuse my saying so."

Clarissa shrugged. "I like to hustle. I've had to. But— Oh, well, you know how it is. I sort of fell for him. I mean, he does have a lot of charm."

"True enough," Abigail bitterly agreed.

"And he did promise me," Clarissa went on, "he'd help me. I run an escort business—companions for visiting businessmen, that kind of thing. James promised me he'd get me all his rich aristocratic friends, and would double my business. So, like an idiot, I supported him to stop him from going totally bankrupt. You realize he's supporting two illegitimate children?"

Lord Barrington groaned from behind his hands. "Lies!" he cried. "All lies!"

"Anyway," Clarissa continued, evidently enjoying his torment. "James was hopeless. All he did, in the past three months, was have affairs with other women—he can't resist them, you know—and run up bills. And none of his contacts were any good, either. His friends are as broke as he is. You've got to understand, Abigail, the aristocracy in this country is just about threadbare."

"Hmm," said Abigail, thinking that this did actually make some sense. "But what about his connections with the Royal Family? Isn't that a source of income?"

"Him, royalty?" Clarissa started giggling again.

"But when I met him in Los Angeles, he was on diplomatic business!" Abigail protested.

"Like hell he was. I paid his air fare over there, because he dreamed up some stupid plan to con some Arabs in Beverly Hills. He was going to sell them phony stocks. Of course, they were too sharp to fall for it. I tell you, Abigail, he's a total failure. Just an upper-class twit who can't resist sexy women."

Abigail was thinking back. She was remembering when she first met Lord Barrington on the grounds of Berman's mansion. Lord Barrington had told her his crown and robes were real—but he'd casually walked off and forgotten the crown while she'd had sex with him. Would any real member of royalty have acted like that?

"My god, I've been totally conned," said Abigail. She felt a wave of dismay as she realized that, until this moment, she'd still held out some secret hope for Lord Barrington. She'd been so impressed by him, she really wanted him not to turn out to be totally bad.

Clarissa sighed. "I know how you feel," she said. Impulsively she took Abigail's arm and squeezed it. "I suppose you and I should be friends, rather than rivals," she went on. "I mean, I hated you this afternoon. But I didn't realize what a story he'd told you. And anyway, I honestly don't care any more, what he does." She looked down at Lord Barrington. "I've really had enough, this time," she said. "Do you understand?"

Lord Barrington raised his head from his hands. He ignored Clarissa. "Abigail," he implored, and stood up and reached out to her. He touched her cheek. "Abigail, you surely don't believe anything this wretched woman—"

"Don't touch me!" Abigail snapped, feeling a sudden surge of intense anger. She grabbed his wrist and pulled it away, making sure she dug her fingernails in as she did so.

Lord Barrington paused a moment. He saw in Abigail's face that he wouldn't be able to get around her this time.

222

Without missing a beat he turned to Clarissa. "Clarissa, dear," he said with a shrug, "I admit I've been a bit irresponsible. But when the thing with the Arabs fell through, I had to do something. It was opportune that I met Abigail. She's extremely wealthy, you know." He gave Clarissa a secret smile. "I wanted to repay you for getting me to America, and I thought—"

"You're wasting your breath, James." She glared at him.

"Oh." Lord Barrington stopped, and nervously straightened his tie.

Abigail watched him, feeling sick. It was beyond doubt now, what he was. That she should have had sex with him was bad enough. But to have been so hung up on him—

"Well, I suppose I'd better go," said Lord Barrington, avoiding looking at either of the women. "Since both of you will believe only the worst of me, I have no recourse but to—to muddle through as best I can." He stepped cautiously between Abigail and Clarissa, and started shuffling toward the door.

Abigail looked at Clarissa. Clarissa looked at Abigail. There was a sudden understanding between the two women.

Together, they turned and grabbed him.

"Just a goddamn minute!" Abigail shouted at him.

"You're not getting out of this so easily!" added Clarissa.

Chapter Twenty-eight

Lord Barrington struggled quite a bit, but he was no match for them. Abigail was mad as hell, and more than ready to act it out. Clarissa had gotten her strength back after tussling with Moira, and James was obviously afraid of her temper.

Within minutes they had him trussed up. Abigail copied Moira's technique, ripped the wire out of the phone, and used it to lash Lord Barrington's wrists together. But instead of tying them behind him, she tied them above his head, and then lashed them to the top end of the bed.

"I shall scream!" Lord Barrington declared. His voice sounded determined and strong, but his eyes were moving nervously. "I shall scream for help. This is a serious offense. I shall sue for assault. I warn you, Clarissa—"

"Stuff it!" she told him. She grabbed his monogrammed handkerchief out of his pocket, then reached inside his jacket and pulled out a ballpoint pen. "Hold his head, Abigail."

Lord Barrington struggled, but Abigail got a good grip on his handsome mane of hair.

Warily, Clarissa used the pen to poke the handkerchief into Lord Barrington's mouth.

He grunted and tried to spit it out.

Clarissa quickly pulled off one of his shoes, took off

his sock, and tied it around his face to keep the handkerchief in place.

"What we need now," said Abigail, breathing hard with a mixture of exertion and excitement, "is a little something from Moira. You remember, what she had in her hand when she chased George around the lobby of the Ritz this morning?"

"Why, yes, I think I do," said Clarissa. She giggled wickedly.

Lord Barrington looked from one of them to the other, not knowing what they were talking about. He made desperate smothered noises.

"I'll slip up and get it," said Abigail. "You stay here and pull his clothes off. If you get bored, you can always tickle him."

"What a good idea," Clarissa agreed. "You know, Abigail, I quite misjudged you. You were so—so snooty, and you were so bitchy to me before."

"Well, you acted pretty badly yourself. Overacted, in fact."

"Oh, it's true. I know I do. When I feel unsure of myself, especially. I do it because it drives the women crazy, and it attracts all the men—"

"Such as Brad."

Clarissa bit her lip. She looked coy. "Well, he was so cute," she said. "And I did so want to steal him from you."

"Well, I hope you know what to do with him, now that you've got him," said Abigail.

"Oh yes," Clarissa agreed quickly. "I have lots of plans." She turned slightly pink. "You don't mind—?"

"He was never really my type," said Abigail. "I just liked having him around, totally devoted to me. For a while."

She was interrupted by a knock at the door.

"That's him now," Abigail said in a whisper. "I don't want him to see James like this. I'll send him up to the room he just reserved, and tell him you'll join him later,

okay? And then I'll go up to Moira's room and get the—
the you-know-what."

"Absolutely!" said Clarissa, with a conspiratorial wink.

Abigail had no trouble dealing with Brad, and no trouble
getting the riding crop, either. Moira was soothing her
abused flesh in the bathtub, with George tenderly massaging her. Abigail snuck into their room, found the riding crop, and snuck out again.

Back in her own room she found that Clarissa had
stripped Lord Barrington totally naked and was sitting
on his chest on the bed, playing with his cock, while he
turned his head from side to side, struggling helplessly in
his bonds, and made more smothered noises behind his
handkerchief-gag.

Abigail dropped the riding crop on the floor beside the
bed without Lord Barrington seeing it, and then sat on
the sheets next to Clarissa.

"He has such a large organ, doesn't he?" said Clarissa,
with a giggle. She trailed her fingers tantalizingly up the
length of Lord Barrington's straining cock, then batted it
lightly from side to side. "And he can't resist being played
with."

"It is large, isn't it?" said Abigail. She wetted her finger,
then traced slow circles around the top of the penis. "You
know, he tantalized me, more than once," Abigail went
on. "That was part of his sex technique. Either he half
raped me, or he made me so horny I almost begged him
for it."

"Me too," said Clarissa. "You think we should give
him a taste of his own medicine?"

"Definitely," Abigail said intently.

"He always did like my breasts," said Clarissa. She
turned around, leaned over Lord Barrington, and lowered
herself toward his head. Though she was still wearing her
rumpled low-necked dress, it revealed enough of her so
that she was able to press the tops of her breasts against
his gagged mouth.

He groaned deep in his throat. His cock strained and grew larger.

"Kiss my tits, James," Clarissa said. She reached behind her, undid her dress, and shrugged it down over her shoulders. She was wearing a low-cut, push-up bra. She undid that, also.

Clarissa's big breasts flopped out into Lord Barrington's face. She massaged her tits across his cheeks and down to his mouth again. "Kiss them," she ordered him again. "Kiss them, or we'll keep you tied up here all night!"

Helplessly he pressed his gagged mouth to the ample mounds of flesh, and made futile motions with his lips, as much as the gag permitted.

Clarissa pulled back suddenly and laughed at him. She rubbed her big breasts with her hands, then jiggled them invitingly. "You won't ever touch them again," she told Lord Barrington. "Never." She rolled one of the nipples between her finger and thumb. "I won't ever let you do this again, either. Because you were so rotten to me."

She squirmed down and trailed her breasts across his chest, then down to his crotch. She squeezed her tits together, and glanced up at Abigail. "Hold his cock," she said.

Abigail did as Clarissa told her.

Clarissa moved so that Lord Barrington's long, fat cock pushed between her breasts. She rocked up and down, and his penis rubbed back and forth between the sandwich of soft flesh.

He groaned once more and twisted on the bed. Abigail saw his balls retract and his stomach muscles clench. "He's almost coming," she warned Clarissa.

Clarissa drew back at once. "We can't have that, can we?" She was breathing hard, and there was a wild look in her eyes.

"Definitely not," Abigail agreed.

"Naughty James," said Clarissa. Without warning she slapped his face, much as she had slapped Moira's earlier.

228

"Naughty, naughty, naughty!" And she slapped him again, much harder.

"You think we should punish him now?" said Abigail.

"Yes!" Clarissa exclaimed. "I'll turn him on his tummy, and hold him." She grabbed his shoulder and pulled him over, so he was face down on the bed. His erect cock was squashed to one side, under his thigh. He tried to resist Clarissa, but with his hands tied above his head he could do nothing.

Abigail quickly picked up the riding crop from the floor. She waved it experimentally. This was Moira's fetish, not hers—she didn't know how hard to hit. But then she realized she should just hit as hard as she could. In view of the way James Barrington had treated her, he could hardly expect any mercy now.

"All right," said Abigail. She stood with her legs apart and took aim at Lord Barrington's naked buttocks. "This is for lying to me in Los Angeles." And she brought the riding crop down.

It made a faint whooshing noise as it cut through the air. It smacked into Lord Barrington's skin, and his whole body jumped. He made a surprised noise behind his gag, and tried to twist free from Clarissa's grip.

"Again!" said Clarissa, her eyes bright.

Abigail raised the crop once more. She admired the thin red line that was appearing on Lord Barrington's pale flesh, marking where the riding crop had landed.

"This is for lying to me about Clarissa," Abigail said. "Your so-called wife!" And she brought the riding crop down once more, using all her strength.

It smacked across his ass, and he flinched so violently, he almost twisted out of Clarissa's grip. He started making pleading, imploring noises behind the gag.

"And this is for lying to me about being royalty," said Abigail. She beat him again. "And this is for grabbing me in your limousine." She beat him again.

"It's my limousine, actually," said Clarissa. "At least, I rent it."

"And this is for lying to me tonight," said Abigail. She beat him again. "And—and this is just because you deserve it, you bastard!" And she brought the riding crop down six or seven times more, putting all her anger and her hurt feelings into it. Lord Barrington flinched and moaned with every blow. The lines on his ass grew into deep welts. His whole bottom turned bright red.

Finally Abigail slumped down on the side of the bed and dropped the riding crop. She was gasping for breath, and she'd gotten rid of all her aggressions. She felt exhausted but vindicated. "Why couldn't you just tell me the truth, all along?" she complained to Lord Barrington. "I could've enjoyed you, anyway." She looked away from him, feeling a brief pang of remorse.

"He's a compulsive liar, Abigail," said Clarissa. "He can't help himself." She surveyed Lord Barrington's ass. "I must say, you covered that area rather thoroughly, so I think for my punishment, I'll do something different." She rolled her captive onto his back again.

Lord Barrington's face was flushed and damp with sweat. He was taking quick, short breaths through his nose and groaning behind the gag. His cock was no longer erect—the punishment with the riding crop had certainly not turned him on.

"I'm going to pinch you all over," said Clarissa, with a wicked smile. "You used to pinch my nipples sometimes—till it hurt. How do you like it yourself, James?" And she nipped his left nipple between her fingernails.

For several minutes she kept it up, pinching him from his nipples to the soles of his feet. Lord Barrington writhed and bucked and twisted desperately, unable to escape. He moaned and whimpered. He looked up at Abigail, as if imploring her to stop Clarissa and end the torment. But Abigail just shrugged and smiled. "You deserve it," she told him quietly. "You deserve every minute of it."

Finally Lord Barrington shut his eyes and turned his head away, as if he knew she was right.

A little later Abigail and Clarissa sat back together,

both of them feeling they had taken their revenge as far as it needed to go.

"Think he's learned his lesson?" said Clarissa.

"Maybe," said Abigail. "Yes, I think maybe he has."

"Well, you untie him," said Clarissa.

Abigail went and started loosening the wire binding Lord Barrington's wrists. "You think he's—er, safe?"

"He knows better than to try to hurt me," said Clarissa. "I grew up in the East End, Abigail. That's a rough part of London. But I got out of it—as soon as I could—and learned how to talk with a posh accent . . . and I learned how to flirt with men and run my own business too. But back when I was still a kid, before anything else, I learned how to defend myself."

"I guess you did," said Abigail, pausing and touching the bruise on her jaw which Clarissa had inflicted that morning.

Then she released Lord Barrington, and pulled his gag off. Slowly he sat up on the bed. There was a haunted, beaten look in his eyes.

"Here are your clothes," Clarissa said, and threw them to him.

Lord Barrington dressed slowly, without looking directly at either woman. He seemed to be trying to preserve as much dignity as possible under the circumstances. Abigail watched him warily.

Finally he laced his shoes and stood up. He turned to Abigail and stared at her balefully. "You are lucky, my dear," he said in a quavering but solemn tone, "that I do not hold you responsible for what you have just done. It is not your fault you believed this harlot's pack of lies." He gestured at Clarissa. "And it is your loss, as well as mine, that you will never know how terribly you misjudged me, and what happiness you could have shared with me."

"Oh, well," said Abigail, "I guess I'll manage somehow, anyway."

Lord Barrington ignored her sarcasm. He turned to

Clarissa. "As for you," he said, still in the sanctimonious tone, "I cannot tell you how glad I am to be free of your temper tantrums, your insatiable demands, and your greed. I must have been out of my mind, ever to consider that you and I could have anything in common."

Clarissa just laughed and shook her head, as if admiring his act.

"I shall consult my solicitor tomorrow," said Lord Barrington, moving toward the door, "and seek advice as to whether to press a suit against you both, for assault and damages. In the meantime, good night."

He gave Abigail one last slow, sad look, as if he still hoped somehow to convince her that she had wronged him terribly. And then he left.

Chapter Twenty-nine

A little while later Brad came down and collected his things from Abigail's room. He still seemed embarrassed about having got so interested in Clarissa, but Abigail didn't let him hang around explaining himself any more. She hustled him out of the room, and Clarissa with him. As far as she was concerned, if Clarissa would keep Brad occupied for the next few weeks, that was the ideal way out of an embarrassing situation.

Abigail went and lay on her bed—the same bed where Lord Barrington had lain, just a little earlier, suffering his punishment.

Abigail stared at the ceiling and figured that things hadn't worked out too badly, after all. None of the potential scandals had leaked out, so far as anyone could tell. Lord Barrington had been conclusively dealt with, so she wouldn't have him haunting her imagination any more. Brad would keep Clarissa out of the way, and vice versa—with the accent on the vice. Moira was back with George, since George had rescued her so gallantly from Clarissa's drug-crazed onslaught. And it looked as if Moira wouldn't be making George jealous any more, since it seemed unlikely that Moira would continue messing around with Berman. He'd failed her in her moment of need, and he'd backed away from her—perhaps because seeing Moira beaten up by another woman had ruined Moira's ruthless, dominant image.

The only remaining worry, obviously, was whether Berman was so disillusioned with Moira and everyone else that he would now want to kill the movie deal they had set up together.

Abigail decided she should call Berman to try and soothe him. If he needed soothing. She reached for her phone.

But, of course, she'd torn out the phone wire to tie up Lord Barrington.

Abigail sighed. She realized she would have to go down to the lobby and use one of the house phones.

She checked her appearance, to make sure the evening's insanities hadn't left her looking too ragged, and then left her room and walked to the elevator.

Down in the lobby she found the house phones and got through to Berman. "It's Abigail," she told him. "Is everything all right, Herman?" she asked him in her gentlest, most persuasive voice.

"Is what all right?" He sounded slightly out of breath.

Abigail frowned. She hoped there wasn't some new weird scene going on up there. "I was just worried about what you said, Herman, a little while back. About how you were getting out, because Moira was too weird. I mean, I hope we still have a deal, Herman."

He didn't answer for a moment. Again, she noticed his heavy breathing. "Well, I'll level with you, Abby," he said, finally. "You and me, we worked together in the old days. I know you, you're okay. But your sister—somehow it seems like there's been too much craziness, and she's part of it. She's got a crazy temper, she doesn't know when to stop, and she won't get rid of that guy George. And he's crazy, too! So—hell, for a few minutes, there, I thought, fuck 'em all. I'll do my movie with someone else."

"Oh," said Abigail. She felt a terrible sinking sensation.

"But then," Berman went on, "then I thought to myself,

234

no, you're on the talk show tonight, looking so good, saying you're replacing Helen Hingley in the star role. We can't keep changing our minds, here. It's been announced you've got the role. We have to stick with that."

"Ah," said Abigail, able to breathe again.

"So the way I figure it," Berman concluded, "I'll just keep my distance from Moira. I mean, Abby, I like dangerous women, you know? But this one's too much for me. No offense, of course."

"Not at all," said Abigail.

"So we'll start shooting just as we planned it," said Berman, "and I'll meet with you and discuss the script. Tomorrow all right? In fact, I'd say come up and let's talk now, Abby, except—well, see, when I decided I was through with Moira, I thought I'd better get myself a distraction."

"How do you mean?" said Abigail.

"I gave the desk clerk a fifty," Berman said, "and told him to send someone over right away." He lowered his voice and spoke closer to the phone. "She's here right now, Abby. She's like a professional, you know what I mean? But the best. English, get it? I mean, the best! Boy, can she whip ass."

He resumed his normal voice and stopped breathing so hard into the phone. "So like I say, I'm busy right now, Abby, but tomorrow, okay?" And then, before she could answer, he turned to whoever was with him. "Yeah, yeah, I'm coming. No, I'm not—ow! Ouch!"

And the line went dead.

Abigail smiled to herself and replaced the receiver. Berman, of course, was just as deranged as everyone else. But at least he knew how to cope with it.

Abigail stood for a moment by the phone, suddenly feeling isolated. Everyone now was paired off, one way or another, except for her. She thought wistfully about Lord Barrington—or rather, her fantasy vision of him, as he had made himself seem.

For a moment she almost thought she could hear his

voice. She frowned and turned around. Someone was talking, over in the lounge area of the lobby where there were comfortable chairs and coffee tables. And the man's voice sounded just like Lord Barrington's.

Abigail couldn't contain her curiosity. She crept across the lobby and hid behind one of the large marble pillars. She listened.

". . . distantly related to Her Majesty," the man was saying. "I suppose I'm something like five hundredth in succession to the throne, if one wanted to be technical about it."

Abigail felt a prickly sensation at the back of her neck. She shivered. Was she having mental aberrations, or what?

Carefully she peeked around the pillar.

The man was sitting with his back to her. In a chair opposite him was a beautiful young woman, expensively dressed, her blond hair falling in carefully sculpted waves around her heart-shaped face. She was carrying a camera —obviously a tourist.

"That's just fascinating!" she exclaimed. "Oh, I think British royalty is just wonderful! Back home, we just don't have anything like it." She spoke in a classic Midwest accent.

"Well," the man's voice resumed, "you know, it might just be possible to obtain an introduction for you. At the palace—if you're interested."

Abigail sidled away from the pillar, craned her neck, and caught a surreptitious look at the man's profile. It was him, all right. There was no doubt about it—the man was Lord James Barrington.

"You mean it?" his female companion exclaimed. "Oh my gosh, I'd do anything if I could actually meet the Queen of England!"

"You'd do anything, would you?" said Lord Barrington, eyeing her roguishly.

"Just about!" she said, and blushed.

Abigail groaned. She turned and retreated quickly across the lobby. The woman's wide-eyed naivety reminded Abigail of how she must have been herself, dealing with Lord Barrington.

And she'd thought that she and Clarissa had actually taught Lord Barrington a lesson. Hah! He hadn't even left the hotel, and he was already picking up some new victim with the same old line. Once a con man, always a con man.

Briefly, Abigail considered going and facing the man, and publicly debunking his pretense.

But no, she'd had enough. More than enough.

She looked at her watch. It was almost ten in the evening, and she was tired. She went and pressed the elevator call button.

A little later she was lying in bed in her room, in blissful solitude. Brad was not there irritating her with super-serious monologues about his acting ambitions. Lord Barrington was not there driving her crazy with love-hate. Moira was not there making catty comments. Abigail was on her own, and, she realized, she was happy to be that way.

She lay back, adjusted the pillows behind her, tucked the blankets around her legs, and watched television—watched herself, talking to Michael Larkin on the TV talk show.

The Best of Bestsellers from
WARNER BOOKS

___**A STRANGER IN THE MIRROR**
by Sydney Sheldon   (A36-492, $3.95)
Toby Temple—super star and super bastard, adored by his
vast TV and movie public yet isolated from real, human
contact by his own suspicion and distrust. Jill Castle—she
came to Hollywood to be a star and discovered she had to
buy her way with her body. In a world of predators, they are
bound to each other by a love so ruthless and strong, that it
is more than human—and less.

___**BLOODLINE**
by Sydney Sheldon   (A36-491, $3.95)
When the daughter of one of the world's richest men
inherits his multi-billion-dollar business, she inherits his
position at the top of the victim's list of his murderer! "An
intriguing and entertaining tale."—*Publishers Weekly*

___**RAGE OF ANGELS**   (A36-214, $3.95)
by Sydney Sheldon   (In Canada A30-655, $4.95)
A breath-taking novel that takes you behind the doors of
the law and inside the heart and mind of Jennifer Parker.
She rises from the ashes of her own courtroom disaster to
become one of America's most brilliant attorneys. Her
story is interwoven with that of two very different men of
enormous power. As Jennifer inspires both men to passion,
each is determined to destroy the other—and Jennifer,
caught in the crossfire, becomes the ultimate victim.

Don't Miss
These Other HOT Books
From WARNER!

For Your Pleasure
from *Warner Books*

___**THE WILDON AFFAIR**
by Roland DeForrest   (G30-207, $2.75)
The erotic adventures of two unrivaled siblings. Whether separated by a thousand miles or by the mere whisper of a silken bedsheet, Dirk and Honey Wildon are never out of each other's thoughts. No danger or delight can quell the consuming passion they share. And when they come together the air runs torrid and the stars blaze blue. Because Dirk and Honey are brother and sister...and a lot closer than lovers.

To order, use the coupon below. If you prefer to use your own stationery, please include complete title as well as book number and price. Allow 4 weeks for delivery.